Beyond Forgiveness

Beyond Forgiveness

KAREN ROSSI

A Karen Rossi Romance

Wisteria Publications

Wisteria Publications
507-4 Briar Hill Heights
New Tecumseth, ON
L9R 1Z7

Beyond Forgivness
ISBN: 978-1-988763-17-0
Copyright © 2018 by Kaarina Brooks

Published in Canada 2018

Layout and Cover Art by Taria van Weesenbeek

Please contact the author at brooks.kaarina@gmail.com for any questions or comments.

Dedication

To My Brian

Other Books by Karen Rossi

Acknowledgements

I want to thank my sister Raili for her great editing and Taria van Weesenbeek for her work on the layout and cover design.

Chapter One

"C'mon, Mom, let's get going!"

A photograph on the wall of the church narthex had caught Katharine's attention and she pushed her way through the throng of wedding guests to have a closer look. Mesmerized, she stared at the last face in a row of photos.

Beside her Maggie squirmed, clutching her bubble-blower. "Linda and Ray'll be gone before I get a chance to blow any bubbles at them."

"Just a minute, sweetie." Katharine placed a placating hand on her daughter's shoulder.

"Reverend Bradley Scott" she read on the plaque under the photo of the young minister. There was something about his intense, dark blue eyes that would have made it impossible for Katharine to turn away, even if the whole Redemption Church had come crashing down on her head.

The man was probably making a serious effort to appear benevolent and holy, with his fair hair combed back to look sober, but somehow he managed to look un-pastorly, giving the appearance that, at any moment, a few unruly strands could tumble onto his forehead. She imagined how the hair would look, wind-blown and tousled, with her hand brushing it off his forehead.

The strong jaw was freshly-shaven, glistening smooth. How would it feel to kiss him with a day's growth of beard? Katharine refused to feel blasphemous. So what if he was a man of the cloth? He was still human, wasn't he? And handsome as the devil. "Mom!" Maggie squealed. "If we don't get going, we'll be locked up here for the night."

Katharine shook her head and looked around. Enough daydreaming, already. The narthex of the little church was almost empty save for the two of them, as everyone had joined the happy couple out on the church lawn

"Sorry, honey," she said, patting her daughter's shoulder. "I was just reading all the writing under this portrait, see?" Yeah, right, sure she was. But she could hardly tell Maggie she was drooling over the pastor.

Maggie studied the photo, temporarily forgetting her concern about being incarcerated in the church.

"Reverend Bradley Scott. Nice-looking man," she mused.

"Amen." Katharine sighed.

"But he wasn't the one who married Linda and Ray."

"No. Maybe he was away today and couldn't perform the ceremony. Or something."

"But look at *that* man. He sure looks old," Maggie commented, pointing at another photo. "Is that the year he died?" She indicated the last date under the picture.

They had visited so many historical monuments and cemeteries on their holidays it was natural for Maggie to think the last date under a picture stood for the year of death.

"No. Those dates only tell when he was at this church," Katharine told her. "He may not even be dead."

Maggie sighed. "I wish they wouldn't keep changing their minds about these date things." Again Katharine looked up at the dark, fascinating eyes of Pastor Scott.

Good thing he wasn't an ordained priest, or a monk or something, because then he'd be totally out of her reach.

Katharina snorted at her ridiculous thoughts. Out of her reach? As if she was out to get him, for God's sake.

"What's so funny, Mom?"

Katharine grimaced. Maggie was always too quick to catch her moods. "I was just smiling at some silly thoughts." That was a mistake.

"What silly thoughts?"

"Oh, just something."

"Tell me."

"It's nothing."

"C'mon, tell me."

Being a mother and a primary teacher, Katharine had become good at thinking on her feet. "I was just remembering the way Ray looked so nervous at the altar, waiting for Linda."

"You were not."

Drat the child's clairvoyance. "Can't a person have any private thoughts?" Katharine snapped, half-irritated, half-amused. The determined little terrier seemed to be taking after her mother.

"Not if they're so funny you have to smile out loud. You always say people should share joyful stuff and spread happiness around the world," Maggie recited smugly.

"Oh, shush already." Katharine gave her daughter a playful backhanded slap on the shoulder. "What I said is that the *media* should sometimes report happy news, and not always the bad stuff."

Seeing the obstinate look on Maggie's face, she knew enough to give in. "I was just thinking it's a good thing pastors aren't priests or monks."

"And?"

"That's it." Katharine had to laugh at her daughter's crestfallen face.

"Your sense of humor is getting weirder all the time, Mom." Maggie turned away, pouting.

"You see? It's not always worth probing into other people's thoughts."

Maggie was already eleven, but it was still easy to distract her with something funny. Like now.

Katharine pointed to the first photograph in the row. "Look, Maggie. This man is called Thomas Mc-Master. He was the first pastor of this church when it was founded. I think he was chosen because his name rhymes with 'pastor'. Pastor McMaster."

Maggie giggled. "That's funny. So is that when he died?" She pointed to the last date, not willing to give up on her death date theory.

"Perhaps. Or maybe he just transferred to another church, or retired. Then came James Hood. He was good."

"That's why they chose him, right?"

"Right. 'James Hood, the Good'. Then came Marvin Cook."

"So, why'd they choose him?"

"Because his name rhymes with 'the Good Book'. Marvin Cook reads the Good Book."

"What's the Good Book?" Maggie wanted to know.

Katharine was taken aback. "Why, it's the Bible, of course. The Bible is also called the Good Book. Didn't you know that?"

"How should I know that? You've never told me."

Yes, how *did* people learn all those religious facts? How had *she* learned about them? In church, of course. "True enough," she then conceded. "I guess I haven't."

"And he died in 1975?" Maggie stuck to her guns.

Katharine sighed in resignation. "Maybe. Or he re-tired, or went to another church. And this is Henry Hall, who answered the call. He's the one who married Ray and Linda."

"He can't be the same one," Maggie observed. "That

man today was totally so old-looking."

"He's maybe old now, but this photo was taken some time ago."

"But why do they call all of them reverends?"

Again Katharine was surprised by Maggie's innocent question. She took it as a sign of her own shortcomings. "It means they are honored and respected," she explained.

"Why?"

"Because they—" Katharine stopped. How did one explain everything behind that word to a child who was totally ignorant of church affairs? "Because they're good people. They teach good things."

"From the Good Book?"

"Yes, from the Good Book. You got it, sweetie." What a smart daughter she had, able to put two and two together so fast. "But now we better get going to the reception before all the good people eat all the good food."

Arm in arm they strolled into the unseasonably warm late April sunshine, down the wide cement steps, and over to their car, parked across the street.

Maggie preened at her reflection on the shiny car door. "Don't we look elegant and beautiful in our brand-new outfits?"

"We're gorgeous," Katharine agreed. "But I think we look slightly plumper now. Whatever happened to us inside that church?"

Maggie giggled and puffed out her cheeks at the convex reflection. But then she looked up at the "No Parking" sign on the post beside their car and wagged an accusing finger at her mother. "You're parked illegally, Mom."

"I know," Katharine said in a dramatic whisper, glancing around. "Let's get out of here before we're discovered."

"Cheating on the law again," Maggie sighed, rolling her eyes up at the heavens.

"Hey, I object." Katharine opened the car doors with the remote and slipped in. "I'm a law-abiding citizen and you know it."

"Usually," Maggie pronounced flatly. She flopped into the front seat and buckled her seatbelt, after primping and fussing with her new dress.

"Don't make me sound like a small-time criminal," Katharine remonstrated, but couldn't help feeling slightly guilty. "I don't spend my days thinking up ways to beat the system. This was an emergency."

Foolishly she'd hoped Maggie wouldn't notice the sign when she'd parked there. They'd been late arriving and no empty parking spots had been anywhere in sight. Now, as she steered the small blue Honda into the Saturday afternoon traffic, she vowed never to park illegally again—if Maggie was with her. They drove in lethargic silence, basking in the sunshine that had heated the car's interior. Katharine opened the windows, letting the spring breeze fluff the wisps of hair that had escaped from her up-do. It lifted Maggie's long, silky strands and waved them like golden banners around the girl's head.

"That sure was some good-looking priest hanging on the wall."

Maggie's words broke into Katharine's own thoughts, which happened to dwell on the same subject.

"Yes, but that was no priest," Katharine corrected her. "That was a pastor."

"Same diff." Maggie yawned and stretched like a tired kitten.

"Well, not quite," Katharine said. "For one thing, priests aren't allowed to get married."

A sudden realization hit her like a bolt of lightning from above. Maggie had never been inside a church before today. She'd been baptized as a baby in her grandparents' garden, but that had been more as an excuse to have a family celebration, than for any religious reasons.

What knowledge, if any, did Maggie have about the Bible?

"Maggie, do you know the story of Jonah and the whale?" Katharine asked, somewhat afraid of what answer she might receive.

"Does it have anything to do with Pinocchio?"

"No, but it has some similarities."

"No, I don't think I've seen it."

Seen it. As a movie? "How about Adam and Eve and the snake?" she asked.

"That sounds familiar. Is it a book or something?"

"Yes, it's a book." Or something. With growing desperation Katharine tried again. "You *have* heard of Jesus, haven't you?"

"Of course." Maggie gave her mother an indignant scowl. "*Everyone*'s heard of Jesus. He's the Christmas baby in the manger."

"Yes." Dismayed, Katharine sighed in resignation. The basis of Western civilization lay crumpled on the floor mats, wrapped in strings of blinking colored lights.

"What is this, anyway," Maggie wanted to know. "A quiz or something?"

"Yes, it's a test of general knowledge."

"Did I pass?" Eagerly Maggie turned to her mother.

"Sorry, but you got an F, sweetie." Katharine patted Maggie's hand. "But don't worry, it's my fault for not taking you to church."

"What has church got to do with this?"

Laughing, Katharine shook her head. "I rest my case."

"Mom, sometimes you are just *so-o* weird." Dismissing Katharine with a disdainful shrug, Maggie turned to look out of her window.

The intercom rang in the classroom, and twenty-two

pencils stopped simultaneously. The same number of little heads turned to look up at the wall-phone.

Annoyed, Katharine rose and walked over to answer it. It would've been nice if the office wasn't quite so quick to use the intercom for every insignificant matter. Instead of interrupting the whole class, most problems could be quickly settled at recess with just a word or two. She'd just finished reading a story, and now the kids were busy—*had* been busy—drawing their impressions about one of the characters.

Katharine picked up the receiver, and the next minute all air was sucked out of her. She gripped the phone for support it couldn't possibly give and then hung it up with a trembling hand.

Turning to her pupils, she gave them a wide crocodile smile. "Continue working quietly, girls and boys." She forced herself to remain calm. "Mrs. Broughton will look in on you very soon." With as much dignity as she could muster, she exited the room, forcing herself to walk instead of run.

She stopped long enough to stick her head into the classroom next-door. Bonnie Broughton took one look at Katharine's face and almost jumped out of her rocking chair, sending it swinging wildly. The book she'd been reading to her pupils fluttered to the floor.

"I have to leave," Katharine croaked. Fear had robbed her lungs of air. "Could you please bring my kids into your class and read them a story, or maybe sing with them, till someone from the office comes to take over?"

"Of course. You just go, and don't worry about a thing." Bonnie's words should have been reassuring, but nothing could calm Katharine's panic.

With her back to the children, Bonnie mouthed, "What's wrong?"

Katharine only shook her head, turned, and began to run, the clicking of her heels beating a tattoo in the empty hall. She threw a twisted grimace at a couple of older boys, who were loitering by the washroom door. They stared in surprise to see a teacher running in the hall.

"Dee-ten-tion!" she heard one of them call.

At the office Katharine arranged for supervision for her class and then rushed into the staff room, where she grabbed her purse and sweater from her locker. Clutching the car keys in her fist she struggled to wrap the sweater around her shoulders while she raced to the parking lot. She jumped into her car and nosed herself into the traffic, giving no quarter to an approaching vehicle.

With the sound of an angry horn in her ears, Katharine sped down the road. Wouldn't it be ironic if she were stopped for speeding while heading for the police station?

It had to be a mistake. It had to be. Her pulse pounded in her throat, threatening to choke her. It had to be.

It wasn't.

Katharine burst into the police station and introduced herself to the clerk at the desk. Her eyes darted around the place, searching for Maggie. There she was, sitting on a bench by the window, downcast and tearful. Other parents had arrived and were sitting with their daughters, looking equally bewildered.

Except for one father who roared, "What the hell is my daughter doing here with these shoplifters? Pickpockets. Whatever they are."

A woman patted his arm, in an attempt to calm him down, while a tearful girl, her cheeks burning, pleaded, "Please, Daddy, don't. Be quiet, Daddy."

Katharine hurried to Maggie who jumped up the moment she saw her and threw her arms around her mother's waist.

"Mommy, I didn't take anything. Honest, I didn't." Ragged sobs tore through her slim body.

Katharine held Maggie against her breast and the

front of her thin cotton blouse was soon wet with tears.

"It's all right, Maggie," Katharine whispered and bit her bottom lip to keep herself from breaking down. She smoothed her daughter's soft, long hair. "I know you didn't take anything."

Did she know? The horrible thought almost made her sick to her stomach. Why was Maggie here? She must have done *something* wrong.

She didn't have to wait long to find out. A tall police officer called the parents together and told them that during lunch break the four classmates had been at a convenience store across the street from their school.

"We were just looking at stuff," Maggie whispered to Katharine. "We weren't gonna buy anything."

But as they'd been getting ready to leave, the storeowner had become suspicious and asked them to empty their pockets. Two girls had DVDs in their possession, and the furious storeowner had called the police.

"He ... he locked the door so we c-couldn't leave the store," Maggie sobbed in her mother's ear. Katharine rubbed her daughter's back to comfort her, imagining how this frightening lock-down would have escalated the child's fear.

"He said ... he said it wasn't the first time kids from our school had taken stuff from his store. He yelled that he was fed up with us." Maggie's tears began to flow again. "But, Mommy, I didn't even know Amber and Jill had DVDs in their pockets until the store owner started yelling. Neither did Beth."

"I believe you, dear," Katharine reassured her. Maggie had always been honest and would never do anything like this. But if she was so sure of this, why were her insides a quivering mass of doubt and fear? Against all odds, she tried to keep her faith alive in her daughter.

At last the officer in charge confirmed Maggie and Beth were only guilty by association.

"I don't want you girls anywhere near that store on school days," he growled in a voice that seemed to emanate from a barrel hidden deep inside his dark blue shirt. This doubled the effect of the warning, and the girls' heads bobbed to show their eager compliance.

Maggie and Beth, with their relieved parents, were allowed to leave, but Katharine felt terrible for the people still inside the station. What if it had been Maggie who stole the DVDs? How would she now be dealing with the situation?

Outside in the bright sunshine Katharine, weak with relief, and Maggie, snuffling and woeful, got into the car and drove off.

Self-pity nibbled at Katharine's insides. She had no one to help her cope with this horrible mess. The other parents had each other, but she had no one. No one. Her already queasy stomach felt even more nauseous. Maybe she should have remarried and provided Maggie with a father figure. After all, she'd had a few proposals over the years. Was she just too fussy, waiting for *the one*? The one who might never come.

Ted lived too far away and had his new family to look after, so she couldn't expect him to be involved in his daughter's life any more than he already was. Oh, if only there were a shoulder she could lean on. Someone she could talk to about the difficulties of dealing with a daughter who was no longer a little girl. Each year that loomed in the future would see Maggie involved with more and more people who might not always meet Katharine's approval.

"You *knew* you weren't supposed to leave the school grounds during the day," Katharine said, attempting to make her voice suitably severe. She looked sideways at the woebegone girl, and had to steel her heart against reaching over and putting an arm around her.

"I know," Maggie whispered. Her eyes were red and swollen from crying, and she huddled against the door, trying to make herself as small and invisible as possible. "I'm sorry, Mommy."

The tiny voice almost made Katharine burst into tears, and she was thankful for the sunglasses that hid her moist eyes.

Mentally she crossed her fingers and hoped that being hauled to the police station had frightened Maggie enough to keep her from taking up with wrong friends in the future. How long would the effect of this experience last? Kids were infamous for forgetting. What if one day Maggie *really* got in trouble?

What had gone wrong with her carefully planned upbringing for her daughter? A good, healthy home-life with rules and responsibilities. Supervision of schoolwork. Sports and music activities for leisure time. Everything had been clicking along just tickety-boo—or so she'd thought. Where had she failed? Her sweet daughter was breaking school rules and associating with shoplifters. Was there anything she could do to prevent something much worse from happening when Maggie became a teenager? The stage of life dreaded by most parents was coming up much too fast for Katharine's liking.

Her head in a fog, she drove toward the uptown neighborhood where they lived in a modest, low-rise condominium apartment. If only she could afford a house in a nice suburban community. Maybe that would help, or maybe she should move up north to live closer to Ted and his family. That's what Maggie was always nagging her about. She wanted to live closer to her dad. That, however, would have been such a huge move, necessitating a job change, and everything.

With her thoughts far from the traffic, she was startled by a car horn. The light had turned green and here she was, sitting like an idiot. She waved an apologetic hand at the driver behind her and hoped she could reach home without causing an accident.

"Bonnie, I just don't know what I'm going to do," Katharine sobbed. An errant tear fell on the hand that clutched the handle of a coffee mug. The busy coffee shop was almost full of Saturday afternoon customers, but Katharine didn't care that they'd taken up one of the tables for the last half hour. She needed to talk.

Bonnie puffed out a long, loud sigh. A short, slightly plump woman with dark brown hair and lively eyes, she'd been Katharine's closest friend and confidante since the day Katharine had come to the school three years ago, clutching a brand new teaching certificate. Bonnie had been able to give her many helpful pointers on the secrets of teaching primary children, and their friendship had been cemented.

"Kath, it's not that bad," Bonnie now said, placing a comforting hand on Katharine's arm. "Really. You know Maggie's a good kid."

"Yes, but she'll soon be a teenager and you know what that means." Katharine took a sip of her lukewarm coffee and made a face.

"It doesn't have to mean anything bad. I'm telling you, Maggie's a terrific kid." Bonnie chuckled softly. "Albeit spoiled and pampered by her adoring mother, but that's not her fault."

Bonnie's attempt to lighten things up didn't work.

"You don't have kids, Bonnie," Katharine said. "What do you know about these things?"

"Oh?" A loud snort followed. "So why was I summoned away from my Saturday afternoon TV to dole out advice? If I'm so ignorant about children, please let me go finish my favorite sitcom re-run."

Katharine knew Bonnie was just being facetious and didn't mean a word. "Bonnie, I'm sorry. You *know* I know you know kids much better than I do."

"Sorry, run that by me again."

"After all, you've been teaching for eons," Katharine said, but at Bonnie's loud guffaw, she held up her palm. "Sorry. Of course by that I mean you're more experienced."

"Just a reminder—I've *only* taught seventeen years, not seventy-seven," Bonnie said.

"I'm sorry," Katharine said again. Her expression remained gloomy. "I'm just so upset and worried I couldn't sleep last night. Lucky for me it's Saturday or I would've had to call in a substitute for today." She took another sip from her mug and grimaced. "I have to get some hot coffee. Want some?"

"A decaf this time. I've already had more than enough caffeine for a week."

Katharine returned and placed two steaming mugs on the round table between them. "I wish Ted could help me with this."

"You know he would if he could." Bonnie took a sip of her double-double. "It's a pretty tall order to expect him to get involved in the intimate daily details of Maggie's upbringing from two hundred miles away. And with that young family of his, I think he's doing the best long-distance parenting he can."

Katharine sighed. "You're right. It's just that I feel so alone. Maggie's only grandparent, my mother, lives far away in western Canada and the only other relative is Ted's sister, but she's also too far away to be helpful. Besides, she's unmarried and not terribly interested in dealing with pre-tee problems." Katharine sipped her coffee and swallowed before choking out the next words. "You know that Maggie's asked—begged me— many times to move up north to live closer to her dad." Her voice wobbled on the last word, and she gulped down some more brew to hide her anxiety.

"Yes, you've told me." Again Bonnie reached over to pat Katharine's arm. "She's never said she actually wants to live *with* Ted, right? Just live closer to him."

"No, she's never said she wants to live *with* him, not in so many words, but I don't know ... maybe she really *does* want to live with his family. I just keep hoping she'll get over it." Katharine brushed a few cookie crumbs off the table. "She keeps nagging me about it. Okay, not *nagging*, but she mentions it often enough, especially after she's visited there. She keeps 'suggesting'," Katharine applied air quotes to the word, "that I should apply for a teaching job up there. I don't know if Ted has put that thought into her head or what."

"Oh."

"Yes. 'Oh' is right."

"I wouldn't want you to move," Bonnie said. "I'd miss you. But that's just selfish old me talking."

"And I don't *want* to move. I love the school and the staff is great. Including you, I guess." Katharine aimed a crooked grin at Bonnie. "So are the parents and everything. And I love the neighborhood where we live. The condo isn't too expensive, but it's well managed and clean and just the right size for us. I really don't want to relocate and have to go house hunting and all that. Besides, I don't know anyone in Bracebridge, and at my age I don't like the idea of starting my social life from scratch. So I keep avoiding the issue, but I don't know how long I can keep making excuses. Darn it all! Relocating isn't small potatoes, you know. But I love Maggie more than any school or staff, and I just want her to be happy."

"I think you're giving too much importance to this. You always want to do whatever Maggie wants, and then you get upset if you can't. I remember a couple of Halloweens ago she wanted to be a fox and you were so desperate when you couldn't find a fox costume."

Katharine snorted. "Bonnie, the child wants to live closer to her father. I think that's a bit more meaningful than wanting a fox costume, don't you think?"

"Maybe, but it shows how you're always trying your darndest to accommodate her. Part of the divorced parent syndrome. You're afraid of losing her to the competition."

"Thank you, Dr. Freud."

"You know I'm right."

Katharine hung her head. "Yes, I know. But I can't even bear to think about life without Maggie."

"Have you thought of getting married again?" Bonnie's innocent question belied the fact that she had shared every detail of Katharine's few relationships over the past three years.

"Bonnie, you know darn well I've thought about it. I just can't seem to find anyone who's right for both Maggie *and* me."

Bonnie wagged a finger at her. "Maggie won't be with you forever, you know. You've got a lot of years remaining that'll be lived without Maggie. You'll be lonely."

There was truth in Bonnie's words, and that made Katharine feel even worse. She lifted her chin to show her resolve. "This conversation isn't about *my* relationships and *my* future. It's about Maggie." She tried to sound determined, but failed. "And I need *help*." At the last word her voice broke.

Bonnie took Katharine's hand in both of hers. "I know," she said with compassion in her brown eyes.

"So do I sound like I'm totally desperate and full of self-pity?" Katharine tried to smile, but couldn't help sniffling.

"Yes."

"Well, I *am*. Damn it all, I *am*!" She gulped down a mouthful of black coffee to hide a sob. "Maggie's probably getting into all kinds of trouble as we speak."

"Cool it, Katharine. Where's Maggie's usually on a Saturday afternoon?" Bonnie's business-like tone kept Katharine from sliding into useless panic.

"Well, today she's visiting one of her friends." Katharine sniffled. "But I wish she were involved in something more purposeful in her spare time. Something good and morally uplifting, like ... like —"

"Like a church?"

Chapter Two

Church? The word sent a shiver of recognition down Katharine's spine. *Of course.*

"Oh, Bonnie," Katharine breathed. "You're an angel."

"Me? Nah." Bonnie grinned. "I don't even own a decent pair of wings."

"I don't think I've ever told you, but I used to belong to a Youth Group in Bracebridge, and for a few years my social life centered on church activities."

"No, I don't remember you telling me that."

"Well, I did. I was an only child like Maggie, and I didn't have an older sister or brother to tattle on me and make me toe the line. That Youth Group kept me from taking up with the wrong crowd. Oh, Bonnie, maybe that's the answer. Maggie could have fun playing sports and games, and listening to a minister tell stories about the Bible. I remember Pastor Winfield always connected the stories to our own lives and made it so much easier to make good choices."

"Yeah, I can see how that could work." Bonnie got up. "You ready to leave now that I've given you the solution to your problem?"

"Yes. I feel so much better now that I have a plan," Katharine enthused. She got up and picked up her purse from the back of the chair. "I knew it was a fabulous idea to ask you to come and chat with me this morning."

They left the coffee shop and walked toward their cars in the parking lot.

Bonnie dug for her keys in her purse and chuckled. "Anytime. Just ask. I've got solutions to the entire world's problems. Except maybe how to find my keys." She groped in another compartment and at last pulled them out. "Since I've known you, you've never said anything about going to church."

"That's because I haven't gone. Not since Ted, that gorgeous, non-religious football hero, came into my life during our last year of high school. He made my church friends seem like a bunch of goody-two-shoes."

"And he smote you with his good looks and got you pregnant."

Katharine grinned. "It wasn't exactly his good looks that got me pregnant. But to be fair, I was not an unwilling participant."

"And you got married right after graduation. Yeah, you told me."

"Against the wishes of both our families, I might add. You wouldn't believe how delighted Ted and I were about the idea of being parents. We were so grown up." Katharine smiled and shook her head at the memory. "Silly us. We were scared, but delighted. Us ... mommy and daddy. How cool was *that* going to be?"

Cool? Grown-up? At eighteen they were such children. To get away from the disapproving eyes of the small northern town, and from parental interference, they'd moved to Toronto.

The women stopped beside their cars, parked side by side, but didn't get in.

"We thought we knew all the answers." Katharine shook her head at their youthful ignorance. "But after only five years of financial struggle, and more than just a few arguments, we agreed to separate. At least we were smart enough to see it wasn't going to work and had an amicable divorce."

"That's more than I had," Bonnie broke in. "My ex and I fought like panthers over every last thing in the house. Lucky we didn't have any kids, or they would've been torn to shreds."

Katharine covered her mouth, laughing. "Oh, Bonnie, that's awful."

"Awful, but true. I'm just surprised the dog survived. Poor old Mutt lived out his years with us co-parenting. One week at my place, a week at his." Bonnie sighed. "Bless his little doggie heart. He loved us both."

"Speaking of survival, Ted and I always congratulated ourselves on how well Maggie adjusted to living so far from her dad after he moved back to Bracebridge. He worked with his father at the family drug store and got his degree in pharmacy on the side."

Had Maggie really adjusted? Katharine frowned as she got into her car and pulled out of the parking lot. Were the hens finally coming home to roost? During all these years as a single parent Katharine had kept hoping things would just somehow naturally work out, but after the trip to the police station it looked like hoping wasn't enough. It was possible Maggie hadn't adjusted at all, because obviously things were *not* just naturally working out.

Katharine slapped the steering wheel. It was time to get proactive and take some corrective measures. Surely it wasn't too late, and that cute little church where they'd been just a few weeks ago for the wedding could be just the ticket. It was just an easy car-ride from their condo.

Perfect. And, of course, there *was* that "good-looking priest hanging on the wall". The one she hadn't stopped thinking about.

Katharine rang up the Redemption Church on her lunch hour. To avoid curious questions from fellow teachers, she'd remained in her classroom to make the call, and now sat at her desk, taking nibbles from her ham and lettuce sandwich.

The church secretary answered, but summoned Pastor Scott to the phone at Katharine's request. Of course the woman probably could have supplied her with all the information on the Youth Group, but Katharine wanted to speak to Pastor Scott himself in order to hear how he would respond.

"Brad Scott speaking. How may I help you?"

For a brief moment Katharine's vocal chords failed completely. His voice was so rich and deep she was relieved to be already sitting down.

"Hello?"

There it was again, like a brush of satin against her ear. Her own voice came out in a croak. "Hello." She covered the receiver, cleared her throat, and tried again. "Hello." That was better. "My name is Katharine Wilder. I wonder if you could give me some information about the youth program in your church." She was pleased with the business-like tone she was able to muster, despite her agitation.

"Of course," Pastor Scott replied. "What would you like to know?"

Katharine pushed aside her sandwich, to make room for a pad of paper to jot down the information.

"Well, my daughter will be twelve in September. Is that the correct age for joining this sort of thing?" Katharine crossed her fingers and nervously twirled a stubby red primary pencil.

"Yes, that's perfect. She would be one of the youngest, but that's quite okay."

Katharine heaved a sigh of relief. If she remembered correctly, she'd joined the Youth Group at around thirteen, but that was so long ago.

"I also wanted to let you know Maggie's knowledge

of ... of religion is somewhat ... um ... superficial." Katharine hesitated, and then blurted out, "In fact, she's totally ignorant about the Bible. I'm afraid the others might make fun of her."

To her relief Pastor Scott didn't sound the least bit fazed by her revelation. "I wouldn't worry about that, Mrs. Wilder. The kids in the Youth Group are a pretty tolerant lot." This was followed by a soft chuckle that made Katharine smile. "And besides, I don't give quizzes on the Bible. The kids pick up knowledge about those things at our weekly meetings, but our main thrust isn't Biblical facts. We have a lot of discussions about life and friends, and I hope they pick up something valuable they can make use of over the years."

Katharine sighed with relief. "That sounds good." Just what her worried soul had been hoping to hear.

"We go on some outings at a church-owned lakeside retreat in Muskoka," Pastor Scott went on. "And in August we have a two-week summer camp there."

"That's great. I suppose it's expected we join the church?"

She could hear the smile in his reply. "Not expected, but certainly desirable."

Certainly desirable? Yes, he sure was.

With a few more words of clarification, the conversation was over. Smiling, Katharine snapped the phone shut and reached for her sandwich. For the first time since that fateful phone call from the police, she felt comforted.

And very hungry.

When Katharine told Maggie they were going to join the church, the girl was less than impressed.

"Why should we?" Maggie demanded. "What's in it for us?" She opened the oven to see how the fries were doing. "I think these are just about done. Don't you,

Mom?"

"I think so. Use the oven mitts." Katharine scooped up breaded chicken chunks from the frying pan and placed them on their plates. "At the Youth Group you'll do new fun activities and meet new people." Would Maggie take the bait and not give her a hard time?

No such luck.

"If we got money for stuff like that, I'd rather join the Willowdale Sports and Rec Club," Maggie said as she pulled the baking sheet from the oven.

Katharine hesitated. "Well, that's a little different." She had to think fast.

"How's it different?" Maggie divided the fries equally between them, and then transferred a few from Katharine's plate onto hers.

"Well," Katharine began. She spooned steamed broccoli onto the plates and handed them to Maggie to take to the table. How could she make her case more appealing? "The sports club is expensive, but the church group is free." Well, sort of.

She could almost see Maggie's ears perk up at this bit of news. The girl's concern for their expenses always amused her and sometimes totally annoyed her.

"It's free? As in no cost at all?" Maggie's voice rose to a disbelieving squeak.

"Well, it doesn't cost much." Katharine took the skim milk out of the fridge and poured it into two glasses.

"So that's why we're joining the church then, because it's cheap?"

"Well, not exactly. It's part of your religious education."

Maggie's face contorted into a puzzled grimace and Katharine tried again. "You know how you take figure skating lessons? And you used to take piano lessons?"

Maggie nodded. "Yeah?" She popped a fry into her mouth.

So far so good. "Well, it seems I've been neglecting

your religious education, and I feel we should start now."

Before Maggie had time to ask any more questions, Katharine told her about the camp in August. The girl was hooked. Thank goodness Maggie was an outgoing child.

"That sounds pretty cool. Okay, I'll try it. But if I don't like it, can I join the Willowdale Sports and Rec instead?"

"It's a deal." Katharine mentally crossed her fingers. "And it'll be good for me, also, to join the church. I probably need to get out more."

Maggie nodded. "Yeah, and not just to school meetings."

"Right. I think we'll both have fun meeting new people."

"So, you need this religious education, too?" Maggie asked.

"Actually I did get religious education when I was around your age. I went to church quite regularly. It's good to review the lessons now and then."

"Why?"

"Because we all need reminders about being good and things like that."

Maggie stopped chewing, and Katharine could almost see the light bulb blink on. Damn!

"I get it, Mom. You're worried I might be turning bad, after that thing with Amber and Jill. Right?"

Touché! Katharine's cover was blown. "It's not that I'm *worried*, sweetie," she stammered. "I just want to take some preventative measures."

Maggie came over and planted a comforting kiss on her mother's cheek. "Mom, you don't have to worry. I know what's right and wrong. Really, I do."

Tears welled in Katharine's eyes. "I know you do, Maggie. And it was silly of me to try to get you to join the church without telling you the real reason. I'm sorry."

"It's okay, Mom," Maggie returned to her seat. "And you did tell me, remember? You said it was part of my religious ed. You just didn't tell me what religious ed was about. Like learning to be good and stuff like that."

"You're right. But it's not only about that, you know. At the Youth Group they'll talk about growing up and learning to deal with new situations." Katharine reached across the table to grasp Maggie's hand. "So now that you know, do you still want to join?"

Maggie picked up the last fry from Katharine's plate. "Yup. I think it's worth a try, anyway."

Katharine washed the dishes, deep in thought. It was now up to the church to make it interesting enough for Maggie to stay with the program. Although she'd been inside it only once, she had a feeling this church had a congregation that took pride in its place of worship and looked after it with care. It was such an attractive old church with a tall, steeple, topped with a cross that tried to thrust itself high into the sky. Even the narrow, stained glass windows gave the impression that, despite its size, the little structure was straining with every worn red brick to reach the heavens.

Katharine couldn't believe she was concentrating on clothes for a whole week, but she couldn't stop thinking about what to wear to church. She wanted to be modest, but not dowdy. Youthful, but still classy. She was only just over thirty, after all, so could anyone blame her for wanting to take full advantage of her looks? First impressions were important and she'd be meeting a lot of new people. Who knew, maybe Mr. Right—that special someone for her *and* Maggie—was holding a place for her beside him in a pew. Or maybe—and she had to admit this was something she was *really* hoping for—maybe Mr. Right would turn out to be Pastor Scott himself.

She found it difficult to choose from her rather meager wardrobe so finally, to Maggie's horror, she ended up buying a whole new outfit.

Maggie inspected the contents of the department store bags on the kitchen table. "Gosh, Mom, you didn't go out and buy new clothes just for going to church, did you?"

Katharine huffed. "I did, indeed." The child was such a miser. Obviously took after her father.

Later, when she strutted into Maggie's room modeling her new outfit, the girl changed her tune.

"I guess it was okay to spend the money," Maggie conceded. "I think you're the most beautiful mom in the whole world."

"Thank you, sweetie." Katharine gave her daughter a kiss on the cheek. "And I have the dearest, most beautiful daughter in the whole world."

She twirled in front of Maggie's full-length mirror. Yes, she did look nice. Alluring, even. The long-sleeved silk blouse in a pastel hue softly draped her full breasts, and the dark skirt showed off her slim waist and the curve of her hips. While punching in her PIN numbers, Katharine had told herself no one in church could possibly find fault with this outfit even if it did make her look a bit sexy. Besides, it would also be good for wearing to school functions and even some parties.

"I love you, you love me, we're the perfect family." Maggie sang and clowned around in her furry purple slippers.

Yes, a family they were, but perfect they definitely were not. Katharine was only coping, as was obvious from the recent events, and she was pinning her hopes on the "good-looking priest hanging on the wall" in Resurrection Church.

She hoped he wouldn't let her down.

Brad knelt by the small table in the sacristy, supposedly in prayer and meditation. A tall candle on a brass candlestick cast an unflickering glow in the small, windowless room. A suffocating, small room. He hated it.

He rested his forehead on his crossed hands as he tried to focus on his job as a minister, rather than on his own shortcomings.

And on his guilt.

As always during these so-called reflective moments, his thoughts refused to stick to heavenly matters. This meditation was supposed to get him ready to preach the sermon by directing his thoughts toward God, but it always ended up, instead, pointing an accusing finger at him.

Ann. Her face appeared without fail whenever he was on his knees in this prison-like cell. Maybe he should dispense with these quiet contemplative moments and just march into the church and kneel before the altar for a while. That way he wouldn't feel like some hypocrite by the time he faced the congregation.

He had no right to be preaching, especially about forgiveness. He couldn't forgive himself even if Saint Peter in person were to give him an absolution. Every time the word "sin" came up in his sermons—which was remarkably often—it made him want to shout to the people to not believe a word he said because he was the worst of the worst. He was a hypocrite, a horrible sinner, a child-murderer. Not deserving of God's forgiveness.

Brad shook his head and rose with difficulty. All this kneeling was beginning to take its toll on his knees and he wasn't even middle-aged yet. He slumped into a hard wingback chair with its cracked leather upholstery. Even the chairs in this room were uncomfortable, and rightly so. It wasn't meant to be a place where one sat in relaxed comfort, absently contemplating the pleasures of this world. It was a place to come face to face with one's sins.

Which he did with amazing ease. He could contemplate those sins till the cows came home, but he could never earn forgiveness for them. So why should he put himself through all this discomfort Sunday after Sunday, year after year?

It was like talking to a blank wall whenever he tried to pray. Worse. At least a blank wall might give back some semblance of an echo, whereas there wasn't even a tremor of response when he prayed. Only a dead silence that made him want to bang his head against the wall, just to hear some answering clunk in his brain.

He smirked. Wouldn't it look great if Pastor Scott came out of the sacristy with his head full of bluish lumps and a glazed look in his eyes?

The smirk dried up and once again the feeling of despair filled him. Oh, how he wanted the relief of forgiveness from Ann! But that was never going to happen. Ann would never see him and hear him out. In the past he'd tried often enough, but she was gone out of his life for good. Amen. End of story. He was condemned to drag these chains of guilt like some ghostly Mr. Marley.

Wasn't he being humorous today?

Enough of this. Brad glanced at his wristwatch and sighed. Again, nothing had been resolved in this so-called moment of prayer and meditation. Time to rise and exit from the safety of this hideaway and face all those good people who looked up to him and trusted him.

As he rose, the slippery satin stole slid off his shoulders and slithered to the floor. Brad shuddered as he picked up the blood red garment. He replaced it around his neck, where it felt much heavier than such a slip of cloth ever should. Then he squared his shoulders and pasted on his Pastor Scott face before walking with purposeful steps through the little door of the sacristy.

The hushed murmurs of his parishioners greeted him and he knelt briefly at the altar and offered up a silent prayer. "Please help me to not let down these people." He got up and sat down on the side bench for the opening hymn and heard the familiar collective rustling as the pages of the hymnals were flipped. Cantor Jones played the opening bars on the organ and the singing began.

That gave Brad a moment to let his eyes scan the sea of faces before him. Well, maybe not exactly a sea, but he couldn't help feeling good about the number of people who came to the Sunday services. He'd been told more than once how the numbers were up, with new members joining the church. Any new faces today? How about the woman who called him earlier in the week about her little girl? Was her family here today?

As Brad gave his sermon from the pulpit he looked at all the people before him. He wanted to show he really was speaking to each one, personally.

Yes, today there were two new faces—a woman and a young girl. For one fleeting moment his eyes locked with the woman's and Brad gave a slight involuntary start. He lowered his head, and coughed to cover the pause in the sermon, but he knew it hadn't gone unnoticed. There was a shuffle in the congregation as he searched for his place on his notes.

Rats! What on earth made him do that? Those eyes of hers, they touched him somehow. Was there an air of anxiety in them, or was he imagining things? Maybe it was just the result of too much time spent in the gloomy sacristy on his aching knees. He scanned the choir loft where Sandy was seated in the soprano section and, as usual, she gave him a cheerful smile and a small wink.

During the rest of the sermon—even at the risk of losing his place again—Brad allowed himself a few stolen glances at the new visitor with the aquamarine

eyes. He simply couldn't help himself. Perhaps she was
the one who'd phoned earlier in the week about the
Youth Group, because there was a young girl sitting
beside her. The one who didn't know anything about
the Bible. But where was her husband?

Chapter Three

Katharine had been able to persuade Maggie to settle for the fifth row on the left, instead of marching straight up to the front pew so she could see what was going on. That turned out to be a good choice, for it afforded her the advantage of being able to observe Pastor Scott when he delivered the opening liturgy in that deep, sexy, and resonant voice of his.

When he stood in the pulpit preaching the sermon, Katharine kept her eyes glued on him. She found him fascinating. Then, as his eyes scanned the congregation, they suddenly met hers, and paused. Although there were at least a hundred other people looking up at him, she felt that in those few heartbeats his total attention was on her. A tremor went through her, for in that fleeting moment, she saw a glimmer of interest in his eyes.

Several times during the sermon, after his eyes had taken a tour around the congregation and the choir loft, they stopped to rest on her for just a split second. Yes, she could tell Pastor Scott was very aware of her presence.

"Mom," Maggie whispered during next the hymn, tapping Katharine's arm and breaking into her thoughts. "What was the man talking about when he was up there in that box?" She pointed at the pulpit.

"I know he was speaking English, but I didn't get any of it."

"Yes, I know, sweetie," Katharine whispered back. "Sometimes it's difficult to understand these sermons."

When she was little, she hadn't understood them, either. She'd always groaned when the pastor mounted the pulpit. She knew his ascent would be followed by twenty minutes of dreary, incomprehensible droning that felt like two long hours to a kid. The final amen had been like a key that unlocked the prison doors and signaled the start of more singing.

"Why don't they speak so people understand?" Maggie asked from the side of her mouth.

"Shh. Later," Katharine whispered back.

When Pastor Scott stood up to lead the closing liturgy, Katharine responded to his chanting, parroting words learned in childhood.

"Let us bless the Lord," he sang.

"Thanks be to God," Katharine responded.

"The Lord Almighty bless us, and direct our days and our deeds in his peace."

"Amen."

"How come you know all that?" Maggie whispered, eyes wide with respectful surprise.

"I remember," Katharine replied under her breath and added a silent thank you to her grandmother for dragging her to church now and then, after winning the battle of wills with her. To be truthful, Katharine hadn't really resented the outings, for aside from being able to wear her prettiest dress and her black patent leather shoes with ankle straps, she'd enjoyed the hymn singing and the way the congregation responded to the pastor's singsong voice. It was only the incomprehensible, dull sermons she'd resented.

Today, however, she didn't want the service to end. It had been almost magical to take part in the proceedings again, after an absence of so many years. The organ music had brought tears to her eyes and the old hymns had made her feel as though her grandmother were sitting beside her in the pew, instead of Maggie, whose big, cornflower eyes sometimes looked puzzled and perplexed, sometimes were wide with awe and wonder.

"I never knew people did this kind of stuff," Maggie whispered to Katharine at one point. "It's kinda cool."

Too soon, however, Maggie and Katharine were on their way out. They followed the people filing down the aisle toward the doors leading to the narthex, accompanied by a low murmur of conversation. Pastor Scott stood there, greeting the members of the congregation and Katharine felt almost nervous at the thought of shaking his hand. Surreptitiously she wiped her right hand on her skirt to ensure there was no dampness to spoil their first contact.

"How do you do?" All at once his voice was speaking to her, greeting her, hand outstretched. His eyes looked directly into hers and she found herself engulfed by their blue darkness. Then his fingers grasped hers and a warm glow passed through his hand into her. It warmed her very heart and spread through her whole body like a comforting blanket on a cold night. She had the feeling if she could just keep holding his hand, all her worries would be passed to him and be taken care of, and everything would be all right.

Standing so close to him, she discovered that at eye-level his broad chest looked so comforting that for a moment she had the crazy urge to press her head against it, certain to find solace. The thought left her breathless, and she hoped her voice wouldn't fail when she introduced herself.

"Hello, Pastor Scott. I'm Katharine Wilder." Good. There was no observable wobble in her words. "And this is Maggie." She pulled the girl up beside her. "I spoke to you about the Youth Group a few days ago."

"Oh, yes. I remember, Mrs. Wilder." He smiled and Katharine's knees went weak. What an incredibly gorgeous smile.

"I'm pleased to meet you, Maggie." He released Katharine's hand and shook Maggie's. "I look forward to seeing you at the meetings on Tuesdays."

It was over. With a nod to Katharine, he turned to greet the next person in line. In a daze Katharine walked toward the office to pick up their application forms for church membership, only distantly aware of Maggie's chatter beside her. She made brief sounds of assent at what she hoped were appropriate moments.

The contact had been so brief, but its effect on her was incredible. Had she ever felt this stirred, this moved, just shaking hands with a man?

Driving home, she tried to relive the wonderful, warm feeling of comfort that had coursed through her when he'd held her hand, and for a while she didn't want to touch anything with her right hand for fear of dispelling the lingering feeling of trust and security his grip had produced.

Katharine hoped he would make a positive impact on Maggie. He certainly had made a very positive impact on Maggie's mother, to the point where thoughts of him kept interfering with her schoolwork that evening. She was trying to write up lesson plans for the following week but several times caught herself absently stroking her right hand.

That night, the faint blush of dawn was coloring the eastern sky, before she'd pushed his image out of her brain and had fallen asleep.

"I'll come in with you, if you wish," Katharine said to Maggie as she pulled into the church parking lot. It was Tuesday, and the first meeting of the Youth Group.

"I do wish," Maggie replied. "But only just this once. I don't want them to think I'm some kind of a baby who —"

"I get it, I get it," Katharine interrupted. "So just this

once. Besides I thought I'd drop off our applications, if someone's there to take them."

A few kids were already in the downstairs assembly hall that also served as the gym. Basketball hoops were at each end of the room and markings had been painted on the floor. The kids greeted Maggie with grins and waves of welcome. Then someone tossed the basketball her way and Maggie, who played in the schoolhouse league, caught it without hesitation and started to dribble it toward one of the hoops.

Katharine smiled with relief. The gesture had done its job and had as good as ensured Maggie would want to come here again.

For a few minutes she looked at the kids running and bouncing the basketball, and it suddenly struck her Maggie was taller than many of the kids. Pastor Scott had said Maggie would be one of the youngest in the group, but she certainly wasn't the shortest. She really *was* growing up fast. The thought set the alarm bells ringing again in Katharine's head. Maggie was almost a teenager.

Katharine shuddered, recalling the police station episode. Now—she hoped—things were going to be all right. Maggie was in the right place.

"Hey, Pastor Brad, catch!"

Something whizzed past Katharine's head and instinctively she ducked.

"Watch it, Justin. You nearly made our visitor lose her head."

Pastor Scott had entered the room behind her and now walked up to Katharine with long strides. "I'm sorry about that, Mrs. Wilder. We don't usually try to knock our guests off their feet." He turned to the offender. "Do we, Justin?"

"Sorry." The boy walked over, trying to look remorseful. "I guess my aim wasn't too good."

Katharine raised a skeptical eyebrow. "No, I guess it wasn't, seeing as how you missed my head. Next time try to be more accurate."

With a guffaw, Justin loped off to rejoin the game. Katharine heard a deep chuckle beside her and turned to face Pastor Scott.

He held out his hand. "How are you, Mrs. Wilder? It's nice to see you again."

His firm grip made Katharine's heart give a quick skip of pleasure. It was wonderful to feel his fingers once again encircling hers, and although this time there was no long line of people waiting to greet him, unfortunately the handshake was just as brief as before.

"I brought the application papers." She dug the forms out of her purse and handed them to him.

"I'm glad you still consider joining after that near decapitation," Pastor Scott said with a smile. He folded the papers and stuck then in the back pocket of his jeans.

"I don't scare off easily," Katharine replied. Then she became serious. "Especially since I have a lot riding on this." She nodded toward Maggie, who once again had control of the ball and was dribbling it toward a basket, chased by half a dozen kids.

Before her eyes the man transformed from an easygoing youth leader into a kind pastor whose eyes reflected concern. "Want to talk about it some time?"

"Yes, please," Katharine replied. "Whenever it's convenient for you."

"I left my appointment book up in my office, but please give me a call and we can arrange something."

"I will. Thank you." At that moment, she caught sight of his ring finger. Nice and bare. Her heart gave a totally unreasonable lurch of pleasure.

What was so good about that? It didn't have anything to do with this issue. But her heart ignored the voice of logic and she allowed herself to enjoy a moment of illogical happiness brought on by this revelation.

A victorious whoop from one of the youngsters dropped Katharine back down to earth again. "I shouldn't be holding you up," she said. "You have the group to deal with."

"It's all right. Sandy should be here any minute to help out." Brad glanced at his wristwatch. "But I guess you're right. I better get the meeting started. Please give me a call and we'll arrange to talk."

With that he called the young people over to the long table on one side of the room, leaving Katharine to make her own way out.

Just as she was going through the side door, a beautiful young woman rushed in. Her short, blonde hair curled around her cherubic face and she excused herself breathlessly as she brushed past Katharine.

"Hi, everyone!" Katharine heard her call. "Sorry I'm late, Brad."

"That's okay," he replied. "We're a bit late getting started, anyway." Then he called to Katharine over his shoulder, "I forgot to tell you, we go till eight-thirty."

Just as she was closing the door, Katharine saw the woman touch Brad's shoulder in an intimate way before she sat down beside him.

She frowned as she walked to her car. Who was that cute little woman? A very close and intimate friend, judging from her actions. Or maybe even more than a friend. Hmm?

Katharine spent some time at her desk working on lesson plans, and two hours later she was once again sitting in her little blue Honda in the church parking lot.

Soon after eight-thirty Maggie dashed out the side door of the church and flung herself into the front seat.

"Mom," she began, in breathless enthusiasm. "I had *so* much *fun*."

"That's fabulous," Katharine said. So Maggie was hooked. One worry off her mind.

"Did you meet Sandy before you left?" Maggie buckled her seatbelt and turned toward her mother, her eyes sparkling.

Katharine started the car and drove out onto the street. "I didn't exactly meet her formally, but I passed a woman at the door. I assume that was Sandy?"

"Yeah, that's her. It's so *exciting*," Maggie's voice rose to a high squeak. "The girls told me she and Pastor Brad are going to be *married*. Can you believe it?"

Katharine swallowed a lump of disappointment that had risen up from nowhere for no apparent reason. "Why wouldn't I believe it?" Because she didn't *want* to believe it, that's why. "She looks like a very lovely woman."

"Lovely's not half of it, Mom. Sandy's absolutely—" Maggie paused, searching for a suitable word. "She's absolutely fun and fabulous and fantastic."

Katharine steered the car up the hill, toward their condo building. "Wow!" she tried to make her voice as awestruck as possible. "Not only am I impressed with this amazing woman, but I'm dazzled by your use of three alliterative adjectives."

The green monster was raising its head and with the severity of a strict schoolteacher she fought to push it down.

The sarcasm didn't escape Maggie, who snorted indignantly. "I wish you'd stop trying to be funny. Sandy really *is* nice. I mean it, Mom."

In the dim glow of a passing streetlight, Katharine could see the disdainful look Maggie threw at her over her shoulder. Being dismissed by her daughter because of some wonder-woman called Sandy didn't sit well with her.

"I can understand 'nice'," she said. "But fun, fabulous, and fantastic sounds a bit overblown to me." Oh blast it! She was still doing it.

"It's *not* overblown," Maggie countered hotly. "And you sound *jealous*."

Katharine started. God, was it so obvious even a kid

could see through her?

"I'm sorry," she said, placing a placating hand on Maggie's knee. "It wasn't kind of me to make comments about your Sandy. I didn't mean it the way it sounded." Oh, yes she did. "I'm sure she's a wonderful person."

"Yes, she is," Maggie stated, sounding only slightly less offended. "But she's not *my* Sandy. She's Pastor Brad's."

On Sunday morning, Katharine and Maggie marched up the wide cement steps together and entered the Redemption Church. Maggie headed straight down the aisle, toward the front pews on the right side, but Katharine quickly signaled they should sit on the left.

"What's the diff?" Maggie hissed.

"We sat on the left last time," Katharine whispered.

"And?"

"It has to do with left and right brain dominance." The explanation sounded lame. Which it was. It had nothing to do with brain dominance, but with having a better view of the pastor as he stood in the pulpit. Of course Maggie didn't need to know that. Just because the man was engaged was no reason why Katharine couldn't still enjoy looking at the handsome pastor if she wanted to. And she wanted to. "I prefer to sit on the left side in any audience."

Vaguely she remembered having heard a speaker during a Teachers' Professional Development Day give a presentation on that subject, but she had no idea about the facts behind it. However, it worked.

"Brain dominance, eh? No kidding." Maggie was immediately interested. "I wonder which side I prefer."

"Probably the left, same as I. It's hereditary, I believe." Someday she'd have to have Maggie unlearn this bit of nonsense, but for now it served its purpose. They settled in the fifth pew on the left.

As Pastor Scott delivered the sermon, Katharine tried to concentrate on the words, but she couldn't help her thoughts from straying to what Maggie had told her about him and Sandy. She shrugged. Too bad, so sad. The whole point in joining the church was to help Maggie, not to get herself a man.

Beside her, Maggie seemed to be totally engrossed in the sermon.

"That's dumb," she whispered at one point and Katharine gave her a disapproving poke with her elbow. "Well, it *is*," Maggie insisted, but her mother shushed her into silence.

Katharine marveled at the strength and purpose ringing through Pastor Scott's words. It sounded like he had such a firm belief in his message of forgiveness. As he spoke, Katharine noted how his eyes skimmed over the listeners, and wistfully she hoped he would look at her, too.

And then he did. Their eyes locked, and the moment lasted just long enough for her to know he'd been searching for her.

"Let us pray."

If only he could teach Maggie to stay out of trouble, and teach her what she needed to know in order to grow up to be a good person.

"Amen."

After dutifully scanning the congregation and the choir loft, Brad allowed himself the brief pleasure of looking at Mrs. Wilder. Katharine. Such a beautiful, strong name. She was near the same place as last week, and he'd spotted her right away when he'd emerged from the sacristy. As he'd sat on the side bench during the opening hymn, he found himself waiting for the chance to look at her again.

This time, as he delivered the sermon, Brad was prepared for the reaction in his body when their eyes met. The quickening of his pulse and the slight lurch in his chest had caught him off guard last week. Today, however, not only was he prepared, he even anticipated the feeling. It felt good. He hadn't felt it in years. However, it also warned him he was not to get interested in this beautiful woman. When their eyes connected, he had to force himself to turn his gaze away from that forbidden territory. He must seriously guard against getting attracted to her.

That was going to be difficult, because when he'd looked into those aquamarine eyes at the Youth Group on Tuesday evening, he'd found himself almost breathless, feeling like he was drowning in their depths. He'd sensed she trusted his ability to help her with Maggie and, God willing, he would not let her down.

After the service Brad stood at the door as usual, shaking hands. He tried to distract himself by greeting everyone with his usual, genial handshake, but all the while he knew he was waiting for her. It surprised and disturbed him how impatient his fingers were to touch her hand and he wished there weren't such an endless line of people in front of her.

He nodded at Sandy, who appeared by his side, as she often did, to smile and greet the parishioners. She knew everyone by name and could ask just the right questions to make each person feel important.

Then he saw Katharine, and his attention zeroed in on the fact that in a matter of seconds he would be holding her hand. God help him! This wasn't supposed to be happening. He fought to dampen his pleasure and to keep his voice cool and impersonal.

"How are you, Mrs. Wilder?" he said. "I'm pleased to see you in church again." Her hand burned his fingers. He didn't want to let it go.

Chapter Four

The sight of Sandy standing by his side at the door forced Katharine to reaffirm to herself that Pastor Scott's hand was already taken. All week she'd tried to convince herself it didn't matter if he was engaged to be married. She had no claim on him. She'd barely met the man, for God's sake. All it meant was he was not Mr. Right. Yet, all week she had missed the comforting touch of his hand, and she couldn't prevent the unwarranted disappointment from squeezing her heart.

Now Katharine didn't trust her voice, but managed to smile and nod in greeting when Brad took her hand. His touch was a bittersweet reminder of something she'd dreamt about, but his voice lacked all the previous warmth. Downcast, she turned to go on, while Brad smiled at Maggie and placed a hand on her shoulder.

"Nice to see you, again, Maggie."

She grinned up at him. "Hi, Pastor Brad. Hi, Sandy."

It was good he was warm and friendly toward Maggie, because the girl already thought the sun rose and set on him. Katharine gave a shrug. At least someone was happy.

She'd wanted so much to experience again the infusion of security and comfort Brad's firm grip had produced last Sunday. Feeling like a rejected child,

Katharine headed for the door, but Maggie grabbed her arm and began to steer her toward the stairs.

"Mom, let's go downstairs to get some juice or something."

"I'm sorry, sweetie, but I really don't feel like sitting at a table among strangers, striving to keep up a polite conversation." She just wanted to go home and lick her wounded soul.

"Come on, Mom," Maggie pressed, tugging at Katharine's sleeve like a terrier pup. "They've got chocolate cake and everything."

"And how would you know that?"

"I heard a mother tell her kid. She was trying to get *him* to go down."

The implication in Maggie's words was unmistakable and Katharine had to laugh. "Oh, all right, then. Just for a little while."

She followed the bouncing girl downstairs into a large assembly hall where the smell of coffee and the quiet bustle gave the room an aura of warm neighborliness. The tables each seated four, and were decorated with small vases containing fresh spring flowers.

Katharine was glad she'd relented. A cup of coffee wouldn't do any harm, and maybe she could meet a few of the people she would be associating with in the future.

They sat down at a table, Maggie with her cake and lemonade, and Katharine with her coffee. People at the nearby tables directed smiles and nods of greeting their way and Katharine's spirits began to rise.

"I think Pastor Brad's a gift from Heaven," Katharine heard an elderly woman comment at the table next to theirs. The pink flower on her brimmed navy hat bounced in rhythm with her nodding head. "A gift from Heaven."

"You said it, Ethel," the friend agreed. "I don't know if we've ever had a pastor who could lift a poor sinner's spirits like he does. Take today. You just knew that message of forgiveness came straight from his heart."

"Yes, it did, Jean," Ethel said, pursing her downy upper lip. "I felt the same. Straight from his heart it came. And I felt so thoroughly forgiven I could've just floated away on the spot. But I'm afraid any day now he'll get himself transferred to a bigger church."

Katharine was amused by how intently Maggie listened to the exchange.

Jean nodded her agreement. "Yes, I'm afraid as soon as he and Sandy are married, they'll be off."

Maggie tapped Katharine's hand on the table. "See, Mom," she hissed. "What did I tell you? They're getting married."

"Well," Ethel shook her head, making the pink rose dance. "It'll be a sad day to lose him. We all need to hear those comforting words of God's forgiveness. I'm just hoping he likes our friendly little church enough so he'll decide to stay."

"Yes, he's a gift from heaven, as you said," Jean said.

Both heads bobbed up and down for several seconds.

"Don't stare, Maggie," Katharine whispered, although her own interest in the exchange was just as strong. She would have liked to hear more, but just then her total attention was stolen by Brad, who had entered the assembly hall and was picking up a cup of coffee.

To her great surprise he strode straight over to where she and Maggie were seated and laid his hand on the back of an empty chair.

"Would you ladies mind if I joined you for a quick cup of coffee before I'm off to other duties?"

Katharine felt herself blushing like a schoolgirl and stammered an incoherent reply.

"Sure. Sit down, Pastor Brad," Maggie said cheerfully.

"It's Pastor *Scott*," Katharine corrected her. She was

still completely flustered and needed to collect herself by focusing on something familiar, like teaching.

"All the kids call him Pastor Brad," Maggie objected, scowling at her mother.

"It's one and the same," Brad said with a wink at Maggie. "The truth is, I do prefer to be called Pastor Brad. It's less formal."

Maggie's big blue eyes sparkled. She really liked him, Katharine saw to her relief. At least that hurdle had been crossed, and now Maggie wouldn't be nagging her any more about joining the Willowdale Sports and Rec Club. Nor, she hoped, about moving closer to her dad.

As the girl chattered with animation, her long tresses swung in time with her emphatic words. Katharine, on the other hand, sat mute, a silly smile glued to her face. If she'd ever hoped to make Brad think of her as a vivacious, interesting woman, those illusions now lay splattered on the white tablecloth where a brown coffee stain exposed her agitated state. Brad didn't seem to notice, thanks to Maggie's prattle.

"Did you make up that story you were telling about the boy who came home after traveling all around the world?" Maggie was asking.

"'The 'Prodigal Son'? No, I didn't," Brad replied.

"That's good," Maggie continued blithely, "because I thought it was kind of du ... I mean ... not very cleverly written, you know."

Katharine gasped, but then saw a hint of a smile on the corners of Brad's mouth.

"And why is that?" he asked in all seriousness.

"Well, personally, I think before parents forgive a kid who's been really bad they should first punish him, or her, as the case may be. I know, personally, that if I've been bad and Mom *doesn't* punish me—which doesn't happen often, mind you—it kind of like puts me on a guilt trip. You know what I mean?"

Brad nodded. "I think so."

Katharine didn't know how he could keep his face solemn. Only the twinkle in his eyes belied his amusement.

"But if Mom first makes me go to my room, or I don't get to watch TV or something, then it's nice afterwards to hug, or even have a party like they did in that story. Only we wouldn't kill a fatted calf. We'd have pizza." She giggled at her own cleverness. "But, personally, I think the father first should at least have scolded him or *something*."

She stopped for breath while Katharine sat mortified, gripping the purse straps on her lap.

Without missing a beat, Maggie then asked, "So who wrote that story?"

"A man called Jesus," Brad said. "He told the story and other people wrote it down later."

Katharine marveled at the level tone Brad was able to maintain, considering how the corners of his mouth were twitching.

"You mean *Baby* Jesus?" Maggie cried in surprise. "I didn't know he became an author. I thought he was just kind of a Christmas decoration."

Katharine opened and closed her mouth like a beached fish, not knowing how to stop this innocent demonstration of ignorance.

Brad's reply was business-like. "Well, he grew up and was quite the storyteller. Many of His stories are in a collection called the New Testament, which is part of the Bible. You may have heard of it."

Maggie snorted. "Of *course* I've heard of Bibles." Then, to her mother's growing chagrin she added with a smug smile, "Did you know it's also called the Good Book?"

"Yes, I've heard it called that." It was becoming obvious to Katharine he was having more and more difficulty keeping his face serious.

"They keep them in drawers in hotel rooms, you know. I see them all the time when we're traveling."

Maggie leaned over and spoke low, as though she were sharing a dark secret. "But the font is so tiny, I've never felt like reading one." She sat back again. "No pictures, either. It's not a very smart idea to have the font so small people don't want to read them, is it?"

Again Katharine opened her mouth, but closed it when Brad spoke up. "You're right about that. Maybe I'll get you a Bible with bigger font and even pictures in it. You might like to read that." He glanced at his watch and rose to leave. "Well, I must be off to plan an upcoming wedding. The happy couple's waiting." He smiled at Katharine. "Thank you for letting me share your table, Mrs. Wilder. And, Maggie, perhaps the father in the story loved his son so much he forgave him unconditionally. I'm sure your mom loves you like that, too. Don't you think?"

Maggie slanted a bashful smile at Katharine. "Yeah, I know she does. But I still feel better when she doesn't let me get away with being bad."

Brad smiled and put a hand on Maggie's shoulder. "You made an interesting point about that story, though," he said. "I'll think about it."

He walked off and Maggie nodded as she gazed after him.

"He's really nice, Mom," she said. "And he was so funny at the Youth Group. I really like him. And Sandy, too."

Katharine mopped up yet another sticky mess of spilled glue and paint off the craft table. All week long she'd struggled to keep her attention on her pupils, which was proving disastrous when dealing with twenty-two six-year-olds. Never in her career had there been so many upset paint pots and whining children in her class.

Small wonder. Her mind was so preoccupied with Brad. It was infuriating the way his face remained stubbornly before her eyes, and the grip of his fingers stayed imprinted on her hand. Her brain told her to forget about him. He was not an eligible bachelor. He was out of the picture. He was not for her. But somehow her heart refused to listen.

This was totally insane.

"A teacher who has something other than her pupils on her mind should be fired," she muttered to herself. "Or at least be given an unpaid leave of absence."

The pupils had left for the day without tidying up. Papers, pencils, and crayons littered the floor, and storybooks lay where they'd been dropped. Even the book bins were an unholy mess.

Bonnie popped her head in through the open door and wrinkled her nose in disgust. "Ugh, what a mess."

"You can say that again." Katharine dropped a soggy paper towel into the wastebasket.

"Ugh, what a mess," Bonnie repeated.

Katharine frowned at her friend and let out a huge sigh. "I don't know why I allow them to paint at all. This is the third time today I've had to clean up spilled paint. And they seem to think you need a half a cup of glue just to attach two pieces of paper together."

She ripped off another few sheets of toweling from the dispenser and wet them at the sink. With a loud grumble she began to wipe green goop from the floor beside the paint easels.

"What's going on here these days?" Bonnie asked, shaking her head. "Your classroom is usually the showpiece of the school. I'm always envious of the way you get your kids to tidy up and put things back in place."

"Nothing's going on," Katharine snapped. She didn't mean to sound so irritated and in a calmer voice she continued, "It's just one of those days."

"Obviously."

Confessing to Bonnie she was preoccupied with Brad just didn't seem like a good idea. It didn't even make sense to her. Bonnie would tell her what she already knew—that thinking about an engaged man was really useless and she should get over it. Of course she *would* get over it, as soon as her silly heart started to listen to her brain.

Bonnie pulled her head back to the safety of the hall. "See you tomorrow," she called cheerfully. "Or whenever you're back to being more like yourself."

Yeah, and when would that be? Katharine couldn't even remember what it was like, being herself. Her days and nights were taken up with kids, being responsible for kids, teaching kids, reporting to parents on kids, creating meaningful learning activities for kids. And not just dealing with other people's kids, but having to worry about her own kid at home. She was always on call, night and day. When would her own personal needs come into the picture? Like finding someone to love and share her life with. Someone who would share the ups, and help and support her with the downs of life. Who would give her a feeling of security. Who would hold her so tight she would start to feel whole again, instead of torn to pieces like this.

Someone like Brad.

She slapped the soggy wad of paper towels into the garbage. And now this thing with Maggie and those darned shoplifting friends of hers. She couldn't stop thinking and worrying about it. She hated it all. Self-pity took over and her breathing became labored as she stifled a sob. She bent down to pick up a little stray running shoe lying by the wall and looked for the name on the inside. With a puff of anger, she stuffed it into Matthew's cubby where it should already have been with its partner.

Kids. Her whole life was a mess because of kids. If only Ted and she hadn't started to experiment with sex and stupidly got her pregnant. Now here she was, facing a future of raising a teenager all by herself.

If only she hadn't had a baby.

Katharine gasped and covered her mouth with the back of her green and red hand. What a horrible thought. *I didn't mean that. Please, don't let anything happen to Maggie. I'm so sorry.*

She had no idea to whom she was talking, but felt she had to apologize to someone. Tears of regret sprang into her eyes. She was a terrible mother, wishing her own precious child out of existence. She brushed away the tears, but sobs continued to shake her shoulders. No wonder Maggie kept asking her—nagging her—to *please, please* move up north to be near her dad. Ted was a good father and she knew Madeline was a good stepmother who treated Maggie as her own daughter. Could Katharine blame Maggie if she wanted to live with her dad and her little half-sisters whom she adored? Instead of a mother who nagged her all the time about little things like grammar. Grammar, for God's sake! One of these days Maggie would be able to choose which parent she wanted to live with, and then she might announce she was moving in with Ted and Madeline. So sorry, Mommy dearest.

With a whimper Katharine sank down onto the carpet. Losing Maggie would kill her. She had to try harder to be a good mother. The trouble was she had to do everything on her own. Make all the crucial decisions. Take the blame when things didn't go as she'd planned. She pulled up her knees and leaned her forehead against them, forcing herself to breathe deeply and calm down.

After a few moments she brushed away the last of her tears and sighed. Giving in to self-pity wasn't the answer. Slowly she got up off the floor and surveyed the mess around her. She had to get the crayons and books off the floor before the custodian showed up with his vacuum cleaner. With a shrug she picked up another errant shoe and shoved it beside its pink and blue partner in a cubby.

While picking up pencils and crayons, her thoughts circled back to Brad. Why couldn't she find someone like him? Not only did he seem to be a loving sort of man and great with kids, but judging from the comments she'd overheard on Sunday, he was admired and respected by everyone. Including Maggie.

Holding a rumpled picture book against her breast, Katharine hugged herself. It would be wonderful to have a husband like Brad Scott. Kind. Gentle. And beneath that smooth-shaven exterior, she was sure there lurked something irrepressible, something seductive and sexy. If one was allowed to say such things about a pastor. And even if one wasn't—dammit, he *was* sexy. Those dark blue eyes belonged to a man who was alive and exciting. And *very* sexy.

Was that why was she was thinking about him so much? Because he was sexy? And because she hadn't had a serious date in over a year? Katharine gave a shrug. She was still young and vibrant and had the right to dream about sexy men. Even drool over this out-of-reach sexy minister. And she'd certainly done a lot of drooling in the past week. Defiantly Katharine raised her chin. Why not?

Of course lucky Sandy didn't have to drool. She had him all to herself.

Maybe it would help make her stop dreaming about sexy Brad if she accepted Steve's repeated requests for a date. The fellow teacher had been pursuing her for some time now, trying to get her to go out with him, but somehow she hadn't been attracted to him enough to accept his invitations. Steve was nice, but nothing about him drew her the way Brad did. Yes, Steve sure wasn't Brad.

Brad. Brad. Brad. How long would it take before she stopped thinking about him?

With a huge sigh she walked over to the low shelves along the walls of the room and pushed the book with its worn, rounded corners onto the shelf among other equally loved picture books.

Katharine smiled. Maggie had always loved books. When she was a tiny baby she'd literally loved them, chewing on the corners for a quick snack whenever she could avoid her mother's vigilant eyes.

As she passed by the tall classroom mirror, Katharine burst out laughing. A monster with a face streaked with green and red paint looked back at her.

That night Katharine had barely walked in through the door when Maggie, who was bubbling with excitement, accosted her.

"Pastor Brad called," the girl announced, hopping from one foot to the other. "He asked if it's okay for him to come over for a visit."

The PTA meeting had been long and Katharine was thoroughly exhausted, but the news had a magical effect on her. Something sparked to life inside her, though she didn't know why, since the visit would be just another reminder Brad was not for her. But at least the visit would mean a lot to Maggie.

"That's nice," she said calmly and laid her school bag on the kitchen table. "Hi, Beth," she said to the babysitter who was pulling on her jacket.

"They always visit when there's new people in the church," Maggie went on. "To welcome them. You have to call him and arrange a date."

Katharine paid the babysitter before she responded. "I'll call him tomorrow."

Maggie flitted around like an excited butterfly. "He said it was okay to call tonight. We can get some doughnuts and serve tea or coffee or something. Right?"

Katharine smiled. For Maggie the ultimate in hospitality was a box of doughnuts from the nearby "Donut Hole". "Maybe I'll just pick up a cheese tray," she mused.

"No, Mom," Maggie whined. "Doughnuts."

"And doughnuts," Katharine conceded.

"So call him now," Maggie egged her on.

Why was she hesitating? Nervousness, such as she hadn't experienced for a long time, filled her at the thought of phoning him. Was she really so madly infatuated with the man she was scared to even talk to him?

Hello, this is Mrs. Wilder, she rehearsed in her mind. No. *This is Katharine Wilder. I understand you'll be honoring us with your presence.* Good grief, no. *I have a message here to call you about a possible visit.* Arrgh! *Maggie told me you would like to come and pay us a visit.* Not!

After sweating by the phone for an eternity, she decided to bite the bullet and attempt an impromptu conversation. After all, she couldn't go on rehearsing every line she would ever speak to the man.

Brad answered on the fourth ring, just when Katharine was beginning to despair. "Ah, yes, Mrs. Wilder. As I explained to Maggie, it's the custom in our church to pay a visit to new parishioners to welcome them personally into the congregation. I'd like to do that, whenever it's convenient for you."

"Yes, that would be nice," was all Katharine was able to muster, after a couple of deep breaths.

"Is there any particular evening that would suit you?"

"Friday evening at seven-thirty would be fine." Katharine couldn't believe she'd regained her normal voice. Remembering all those sexy dreams she'd had about him, she suddenly felt embarrassed. What if her thoughts could be conveyed to him via some special heavenly connection? Yikes! Not funny.

"Friday will be good," Brad said. He sounded relaxed, and nothing indicated he knew the intimate details of her indecent dreams.

"Maggie has already decided what we'll serve you,"

she told him.

"Please don't go to any trouble, Mrs. Wilder."

"Be assured, it will be very down-to-earth fare. Maggie's absolutely convinced you love doughnuts."

"And I do. Tell her I look forward to Friday evening."

"I will. Good night, Pastor Scott."

"Good night, Mrs. Wilder."

Katharine hummed as she began to prepare an evening snack for Maggie. Why on earth should she be so happy about the visit? It was just a formality, after all, and it meant nothing. Not to him, anyway. And it shouldn't have meant anything to her, either.

But it did.

"I hope Sandy comes, too," Maggie mused, crunching a cracker topped with peanut butter.

Oo-kay then. Katharine's euphoric mood slammed back down to earth.

Right where it belonged.

On the day of Brad's visit, Katharine came home late from school, carrying bags from a ladies' wear store. She apologized to Beth for being late and gave her an extra bill or two.

"Mom!" Maggie yelped. "That's two outfits in just two weeks. Are you trying to blow our whole budget?"

"It's spring," Katharine said, and couldn't keep the defensive tone from her voice. For some time now, she'd been teaching Maggie about the importance of thrift and savings accounts, and now her teach-by-example was in danger of being flushed down the drain. "I'm tired of wearing the same old clothes," she added, but not without a twinge of guilt.

"For God's sake, Mom, take it easy. You're a teacher, not a tycoon."

"In case you've forgotten," Katharine snapped, "you are my daughter, not my accountant. Nor do I need a conscience looking over my shoulder at my every purchase. I'm quite aware of the balance in *my* bank account."

God, didn't they sound like husband and wife! Katharine made a mental note to inspect their relationship at the earliest opportunity, because it sure looked like it was in need of some adjustments.

Their two-bedroom condo was modest, but cozy. While waiting for Katharine to come home, Maggie had set out flowered mugs and matching plates on the coffee table in the living room, after checking every surface for dust. Now she lit candles here and there to give the room an aura of warmth. Her own room sparkled like it hadn't done since the last visit from her father.

When the phone rang to announce their visitor, Maggie jumped up to answer it. "Come on up," she caroled, and a moment later Brad was in the room, accompanied by an elderly woman with a gray, wispy bun. Definitely not Sandy.

"This is Mrs. Ericson," Brad said. "She's a senior member of the Congregational Council."

He was dressed in his usual dark suit and, of course, the clerical collar that clearly spelled out, "Church business."

When they shook hands, Katharine once again felt the warmth that had been there at their first meeting. His greeting was friendly but formal, as one would expect under the circumstances, but Maggie's bubbly presence soon had him looking more relaxed.

They all sat down, Brad in the armchair and Mrs. Ericson on the couch beside Katharine. Maggie sat on the floor by Brad's feet, leaning on the ottoman with her chin in her hands, reminding Katharine of one of the ten disciples.

Whereas in church Katharine had constantly kept her eyes on him, here at close quarters she was only able to give him quick glances. To look directly into those dark blue eyes would have been like looking at the sun without protection. There was an absurd turmoil in her breast and she hoped her silly heart would soon settle down.

After some preliminary chatter about the weather, Katharine brought out the coffee, cheese, and crackers, while Maggie proudly carried in the platter of doughnuts. She placed them on the coffee table in front of Brad.

"Wow, doughnuts! My favorite," Brad exclaimed right on cue and Katharine was delighted to see Maggie's face break into a wide smile.

"Yeah, I like them, too. But Mom won't let me have them very often," the girl admitted.

"Wise mom," Brad said. "Donuts aren't exactly health food."

"Yeah, I know," Maggie said. "But she says they're okay now and then."

"This is lovely, very lovely," Mrs. Ericson chirped in. "You have a lovely home, Mrs. Wilder."

Brad turned to Katharine. "I saw on your application you were born in Bracebridge," he said. "That's beautiful country. I come from North Bay, myself."

"Do you? How nice," Katharine replied. Nice. Couldn't she come up with a more interesting adjective? She gave a short laugh. "Almost neighbors, one could say."

"I was born in Toronto," Maggie announced, not to be left out.

"No kidding," Brad marveled. "Big city girl. But I'll bet you've been to Bracebridge, too?"

Katharine liked the way Brad brought Maggie into the conversation.

"Oh, yeah, all the time," Maggie said. "My dad lives there. And his wife, Madeline, and my two little sisters. Grandma and Grandpa Wilder are dead now, and so's my other Grandpa."

"I'm sorry," Brad said, and Maggie nodded in acknowledgement.

"How long have you been ordained, Pastor Scott?" Katharine asked after the brief moment of respectful silence had passed.

"I got a pretty late start," Brad told her. "I graduated from university with a degree in commerce, but after a few years I—"

His eyes shifted from hers. Then he coughed and went on. "I went into the seminary for three years, and then did my one year internship in Waterloo. I was a pastor at the Gethsemane Church there, until I moved here. That's about it in a nutshell. Not much to tell."

Katharine's alert ears had picked up the slight pause. There was something in his past he didn't want to talk about. Of course everyone had secrets, but what was his? Her curiosity was piqued.

"And we hope Pastor Scott will stay in the Resurrection Church for many more years," Mrs. Ericson broke in. "He's certainly been a great asset to the church."

"Thank you." Brad smiled at Mrs. Ericson, feeling like a hypocrite. He wanted to kick himself. A great asset? Sure he was. The Great Pretender was more like it. Hadn't he just said to Katharine there wasn't much to tell? Not much. Just Ann. And the hospital. And the baby that never had a chance to live. Just some usual life-changing stuff. Not much to tell at all.

Afraid the pain inside him might reflect on his face, Brad bent forward to pick up a piece of cheese and a cracker. "Those doughnuts look yummy, but I'll try these first," he said to Maggie.

"Yeah, they're Mom's idea," Maggie said. "She wanted to have some healthy stuff, too. Actually she bakes really good pies. Especially apple. They're kind of half-healthy." She grinned at Katharine, who reached over to pat her shoulder.

"Why, thank you, sweetie. It's nice to hear you compliment my baking."

Mrs. Ericson wasn't ready to give up on the previous topic. "I know there are many bigger churches that would love to have Pastor Scott, but our church has what many big churches lack, and that's a feeling of closeness and fellowship. We're a warm community," she finished with a flourish.

Brad smiled at the woman. "You're right, Mrs. Ericson," he said. "It's a great little church. But who knows what the future will bring."

"You're looking forward to having a bigger church?" Katharine asked.

"No, not necessarily," he said. "Little churches are just fine. Wherever I am, I'm still serving the same Boss, of course."

"Who's your boss?" Maggie wanted to know.

"My boss is God."

Maggie nodded with pursed lips and Brad tried not to smile. It would be interesting to work with this child in the Youth Group. She obviously had an instinctive feeling of awe at the thought of a relationship with a Higher Being. Like the way she now showed her respect by remaining silent.

But it was the mother Brad found much more intriguing. Irresistible. In fact, he'd been thinking about her a lot in the past week. Too much for a man who had no intention of ever again getting involved with any woman.

So why had he allowed himself to dream about her auburn hair and her wide, full mouth? And those eyes, a lovely shade of aquamarine? Because he couldn't help it. He knew the minute he found himself sitting here, so close to her, it was a mistake to have come. He knew her beautiful, sultry face—and the way the light from the table lamp now accentuated her strong features—would continue to haunt him in the night. He'd looked for some excuse not to come, and had even asked Mrs. Ericson if she wouldn't mind going by herself, but the lady hadn't considered that proper. She would never dream of it, she'd said, almost aghast at the thought. Never. Of course he'd known that even before he asked.

"The idea is for the parishioners to personally get to

know their *minister*," she'd reminded him. "Not just a humble member of the Congregational Council."

Yes, he had to admit he'd made a remarkably weak effort to try to entice her to go by herself. Probably because he'd *wanted* to come. So here he was, face to face with this woman he couldn't stop thinking about.

Brad swallowed. Where in God's name was his mind going? To redirect himself, he asked, "So you and your husband keep in touch?"

"My *ex*-husband," Katharine corrected him. "I don't see him very often but, as Maggie said, she visits him regularly. After the divorce I went to university and got my teaching certificate. It was a bit hectic there for a while, I must confess."

Chapter Five

Hectic? It had been more like totally crazy. She'd had to run to a babysitter every morning with a toddler in tow, work part-time on weekends and, after Maggie was in bed, burn the midnight oil, studying and doing assignments.

"My father died, and eventually Mom was very fortunate to meet a very nice man," Katharine told him. "Unfortunately he lives in Alberta, so she moved there. I don't see her very often and I do miss her help and advice."

"I can imagine," Brad said. "It can't be easy bringing up a lively daughter like Maggie on your own." He reached down and stroked Maggie's hair. "Even if she is one fabulous kid."

Maggie sent a questioning look at her mother, who nodded. "Well, I *have* given Mom a bit of a hard time lately. You see, I was taken to the police station and Mom had to pick me up from there. I was really scared. And I'm sorry I made Mom worried."

A cookie crumb probably got sucked into Mrs. Ericson's windpipe, for she put a napkin to her mouth and coughed repeatedly. This, of course, caused her to excuse herself over and over.

Brad sent Katharine a questioning look over Maggie's head, but she shook her head slightly to indicate she would speak to him another time.

"More coffee?" she said, rising to pour some for poor Mrs. Ericson.

"L ... lov ... ly," Mrs. Ericson managed to reply, followed by another coughing fit.

Katharine didn't want to continue the subject that had so upset the lady, and instead picked up the lost thread. "As Maggie said, her father remarried. But she's an integral part of his new family."

"And we're expecting a marriage in our church soon, too." Mrs. Ericson, finally recovered, simpered with a coy smile. "Aren't we, Pastor Scott?"

Katharine's heart dropped. She didn't want to hear about this, thank you very much, Mrs. Ericson.

"Well, Mrs. Ericson," Brad said with a forced smile. "If we are, that's the first I've heard of it."

Once again Mrs. Ericson became flustered and her hands fluttered in front of her like little wings. "Oh, I'm sorry, Pastor Scott. I didn't mean to let the cat out of the bag."

"Well, I—" Brad began, but Mrs. Ericson interrupted.

"It's not common knowledge," she said to Katharine. Almost in hushed tones, lips pursed together as though she didn't want the secret to escape, she went on, "But *we*, who are in the inner circles of the church, are eagerly awaiting a glittering diamond to appear on Sandy Davey's left hand." She slanted a reproachful look at Brad and shook her head, as though admonishing him for his negligence. "Even if the engagement hasn't been *formally* announced. Yet."

Katharine saw Brad's eyes narrow. "That's because there *is* no engagement," he said tersely.

Katharine's hand flew to her heart to stop the loud thumping. This was getting more obscure by the minute. She could see Maggie's eyes shift from one speaker to the other, confused, but intrigued.

Apparently Mrs. Ericson wasn't going to let go of

such a juicy tidbit. She nodded several times to prove she was on top of things. "No, not at the present time, I realize that," she said. "But it's been understood for some time now that in the not too distant future ... or am I being too presumptuous?"

Brad frowned. "I'm afraid so, Mrs. Ericson."

But the good lady just wouldn't give up. "Oh, but Sandy's mother, Mrs. Davey," she gave Katharine a knowing nod, "is hoping and praying the wedding will take place soon." Mrs. Ericson sounded bolder now, as though *this* piece of information was irrefutable. "She's not well, you know. Cancer." She pursed her lips again and shook her head to show the prognosis was not good. "And just the other day she told a group of us who were visiting her at the hospital, that she is dearly hoping—"

Maggie, who'd been listening with keen interest, now broke in eagerly. "So it *is* true what the girls told me last Tuesday," she rejoiced. "When's the wedding?"

Brad laughed at Maggie's excitement and his frown disappeared. "Looks like everyone knows there's going to be a wedding. Everyone but Sandy and I. She's a very dear friend, but please believe me, we're not engaged."

"Not yet, right?" Maggie persisted.

"Maggie!" Katharine drew her brows together in a warning frown.

"But Mrs. Ericson said—" Maggie stopped as her mother's eyes narrow into ominous slits.

"I apologize for Maggie," Katharine said to Brad. "She's not usually this rude. I'm afraid the girls at the Youth Group have put some very silly ideas into her head." Little giggly girls she could forgive, but this busybody sitting across from her was old enough to know better than to be spreading false information.

"No need to apologize, Mrs. Wilder," Brad said.

"So for sure there's not going to be a wedding?" Maggie asked, her face still in a pout over her mother's reprimand. "I'll have to tell the girls they're wrong."

Brad smiled at her. "We're not engaged. And you can tell them so, for a fact."

"Not *officially,*" Mrs. Ericson persisted, obviously not wanting to concede that her information was pure gossip.

"So maybe one day you will be?" Maggie piped up again. "Right?"

Katharine wanted to put a stop to this, but didn't know how to prevent Mrs. Ericson from bringing it up again and again.

"Nothing on the radar, I'm afraid," Brad said.

"But Sandy's so *beautiful,*" Maggie said ruefully, as though that should have been enough to clinch the deal.

His eyes locked with Katharine's and she saw his pupils dilate and darken.

"Very beautiful," he said.

Katharine's heart gave a joyful leap. The flash of admiration in his eyes was unmistakable and she was sure his words were meant for her. The eye contact lasted only a brief second, but Katharine's heart was ready to burst with happiness. Brad was *not* engaged.

"She certainly *is* lovely," Mrs. Ericson kept chiming in. "She'll make a wonderful pastor's wife. She's so friendly and cheerful. A lovely woman. Lovely."

"I'll get more coffee," Katharine said and withdrew into the kitchen to calm her pounding heart. She could hear the three of them chatting about Sandy's great qualities, but it didn't bother her any more. Brad was interested in *her.* Katharine pressed her hot forehead against the fridge door. That knowledge was like a wonderful, unexpected birthday gift.

She returned to the living room without the coffee carafe.

"Cute blonde curls. I always envy them." Mrs. Ericson said and then broke into a titter. "I hope envy won't make my bones rot, like it says in the Proverbs."

Enough about Sandy, already! Katharine wouldn't have minded if the old gossip's bones *did* rot.

But the lady wasn't finished. "Sandy's such a cute tiny thing, so friendly and cheerful. A lovely little woman. Lovely."

Katharine rolled her eyes. She, herself, could never be classified as little, and certainly not a "cute tiny thing". She was all of five foot eight and big-boned to boot. She liked to think of herself as curvaceous—but was "cute and tiny" what Brad preferred?

"Yes, she's cute, all right," Brad agreed. "And certainly not very big." He held his hand up to show her size. "Just about five foot nothing."

Okay, so "cute and tiny" it was. Too bad for husky Katharine.

"And she's really good at basketball," Maggie enthused. "And funny, too."

"You're right." Brad agreed.

That was *more* than enough about Sandy. This admiration society was getting way too carried away.

"I'd like to have her visit us. Wouldn't you Mom?"

That was the final straw. "Maggie, you're being too forward," Katharine snapped, and was mortified to see Maggie's face fall again. Did she *have* to reprimand the child like that?

Brad came to Maggie's defense. "Not at all, Mrs. Wilder. I could have asked her to come today, but Mrs. Ericson had already agreed to accompany me."

Katharine's opinion of Mrs. Ericson did a quick reversal. Better her than Sandy any day. She escaped back into the kitchen to collect herself as her stomach tightened with jealousy. What was the matter with her? Why was she jealous of this Saint Sandy when she didn't need to be? Saint Sandy was *not* Brad's fiancée. Nor even a girlfriend by the sound of things. And hadn't he just looked at Katharine in a way that showed he considered *her* beautiful?

She emerged some time later, calm as the summer

breeze, this time with the coffee pot. The deep-breath-
ing exercises she'd learned in yoga many years ago had
served their purpose. Her yoga teacher would have
been impressed.

"More coffee, Mrs. Ericson? Pastor Scott?"

"Why, thank you," Mrs. Ericson held out her cup.
"This is just lovely."

Maggie again proffered the doughnut platter toward
Brad. "Have another doughnut?"

"I certainly will. Lemon-filled doughnuts are my favorite." He took a big bite leaving a moustache of pow-
dered sugar on his top lip.

Maggie giggled and bit into her jam-filled doughnut
with the same result. They licked their moustaches
and laughed at each other.

It was the first time Katharine had heard the sound
of Brad's deep, male laughter. It sent a thrill through
her, alerting her senses.

When the visitors had finished their coffee, Brad
glanced at his watch. "I've had a very enjoyable
evening," he said, rising to his feet. "Thank you both
very much for letting us come."

"Yes, thank you," Mrs. Ericson chimed in. "It was
lovely. I always enjoy these visits to our parishioners'
homes." She pumped Katharine's hand enthusiastically.

When Katharine was finally able to extricate her
hand from Mrs. Ericson's grip, she extended it to Brad.
Feeling again his comforting clasp was what she'd
been craving all evening. All week. Forever.

After the wonderful news about his non-engaged
status, she expected to see the same look in his eyes
that had flashed in them earlier, but to her dismay all
she saw was a polite smile that failed to reach his eyes.

"Thank you again," he said. "We'll see you both in
church, then?"

Katharine's happy expectation fell flat on its face.
What had just happened? Was it something she'd

said?

"So what are you going to be speaking about this Sunday?" Maggie asked, leaning against the wall by the door.

Brad smiled. "I'll be talking about how God's grace reaches even those who feel they haven't earned it."

"Hmm, that sounds *kind* of interesting," Maggie mused. "I actually like the singing part the best. But the speeches are okay, too," she hastily added. "I guess."

"Thank you."

"They're called sermons, Maggie," Katharine automatically corrected her.

"Same diff," the girl said flippantly with a scowl at her mother.

Katharine knew Maggie hated to be corrected, but the teacher reflex made it difficult to stop herself. She wished she could, especially now that Maggie was older and less likely to accept this constant nagging about grammar.

"There's no difference that I can see," Brad assured Maggie. "In fact the word 'sermon' has a bit of a pompous sound to it, don't you agree? As though you're being lectured."

Mrs. Ericson covered her mouth and tittered.

"Yeah, like Mom's always giving *me* sermons."

Katharine gave a short, embarrassed laugh. "I certainly am *not*. She's prone to exaggerations, Pastor Scott."

"I'm sure you're right," he agreed. But it wasn't obvious whether he was addressing her or Maggie. Such a diplomat.

Katharine gave Brad her most beautiful, fascinating smile, but failed to get the desired response from him. Something had gone wrong, but she had no idea what it could be.

At least Mrs. Ericson kept assuring her the evening had been lovely. Just lovely.

Yeah, sure it had.

Sitting up in bed in pre-dawn darkness, arms wrapped around her knees, Katharine rocked back and forth trying to sort out the facts staring her in the face. There was no denying she was definitely interested in Brad Scott. Interested? Fascinated by him was more like it. How about infatuated? She couldn't call it love, but the feeling inside her was strong enough to be labeled something more than just a passing fancy.

She stroked her knees dreamily. He was such a wonderful man, and Maggie was totally taken with him. After the first Youth Group meeting, it had been "Pastor Brad said this," and "Pastor Brad did that," all week long. The fact he was a fabulous basketball player didn't hurt his standing in Maggie's eyes, either.

The problem was that although tonight she'd received a strong signal from him showing he wasn't immune to her, yet when he left, she felt he'd been almost aloof.

Could it be because of all that gossip going around the church about his engagement to Sandy? Maybe he was uncomfortable and embarrassed having been put in a spot like that.

Was there anything wrong if Katharine showed him she was interested? He wasn't engaged or anything, although with his good looks and great personality there probably were plenty of other women vying for his attention. Why shouldn't she, too, throw her hat in the ring? Even if things didn't work out, at least she couldn't kick herself for never having tried. He was just too good to pass up and she didn't want to spend the rest of her life wondering what might have been.

Katharine jumped out of bed. Her bare toes sunk into the soft pile of the carpet as she paced back and forth, thinking of a plan. She'd have to tread softly, because a man who preferred sweet, tiny, curly-headed blondes wouldn't be impressed with an Amazon who forged ahead with the determination of an express train. Even if Brad didn't think of her as a prospect— yet—*she* certainly thought of *him* as one. With patience and time, who knew into what passionate longing she could transform that flash of interest in his eyes.

Getting involved in church activities was probably the best way to proceed. She could join the choir, and surely there'd be other church events that would bring Brad and her together.

Having decided on her plan of attack, Katharine calmly climbed back into bed and fell asleep, just as the birds began their morning warm-ups.

Chapter Six

An ominous feeling of dread weighed heavily on his shoulders as Brad walked down the hospital corridor toward Mrs. Davey's room. He felt like he was the one facing a death sentence, instead of her. His stomach was tied in a hard knot, almost as tight as the clerical collar choking him, because he knew this was going to be a difficult visit. Not just because the woman was suffering from late-stage cancer, but because it was *she* who had requested this meeting. That didn't sound good. He hoped Mrs. Davey just wanted to see him in his role as a minister, and her assumptions regarding his marriage to Sandy wouldn't be on the agenda.

He could only hope that Mrs. Ericson—the old busybody—had just been exaggerating everything.

The door to Room 201 was ajar. Brad tapped on it, but there was no answer. He squared his shoulders, took a deep breath, and stepped in. The small, private room was airy and bright with the afternoon sun beaming in on the many floral arrangements adorning the windowsill. In fact, every available shelf and table-top was covered with flowers from her many caring friends whose intention, obviously, had been to cheer her up. Instead, the overabundance made Brad think of a funeral home.

Mrs. Davey lay on the bed, eyes closed, covered by a flannel hospital blanket. Her heavy breathing indicated she was sleeping soundly. Good. Maybe he could postpone this meeting till—okay, he didn't want to say "till she was gone", but the thought definitely did flash through his mind.

Her previously rosy, plump cheeks were thin and shriveled, and her eyes had sunk deep into their sockets. Sandy had told him her mother had only a few months, perhaps weeks, left on this earth.

Though he was tempted, Brad knew it would be cowardly to simply sneak out. He coughed discreetly, and felt guilty hoping she wouldn't wake up. When the cough failed to get a response, he turned to go with a sigh of relief.

"Pastor Brad?"

It was only a whisper—more like a wheeze, but he heard it and turned around.

"Hello, Mrs. Davey. I thought you were sleeping." Brad came over to the bed. "I didn't want to wake you." He picked up her hand. The skin was parchment thin and he could feel every sinew and knuckle against his palm.

"I think I was dozing. I'm glad you didn't leave." She probably knew he'd been just about to do so. "Please sit down."

Brad pulled up a chair beside the bed and leaned over. "You asked to see me."

He still hoped she just wanted to speak to him about her impending death and afterlife, but down in his gut he knew what the topic of conversation would be.

"Yes. I wanted to speak to you about Sandy."

Bingo! Brad swallowed. "Yes? What about Sandy?" He dreaded the reply.

"She's going to be all alone after I'm gone," the woman wheezed. "I worry about that."

"She won't be all alone, Mrs. Davey," Brad said in

his most comforting, pastorly tone. "She's such a personable young lady, she has plenty of friends. And she has her job. She's told me she finds that very rewarding."

"Friends are fine, and a job is good, but she needs someone to take care of her. She's so young and so trusting, and you know the world is full of all kinds of people. Bad people."

Oh, oh, this was it. Brad's throat tightened and he swallowed. "Yes, there are some of those, of course." His voice was hoarse. "But on the whole—"

Perhaps Mrs. Davey detected his nervousness, because she hastened to get to the point. "I wouldn't be speaking to you if I didn't know how fond you two are of each other."

"Yes, we are." Fond, yes. In love, no.

"I know Sandy loves you very much. I'm assuming you have similar feelings for her?"

Brad coughed out his reply. "Of course."

No, he wasn't lying, because he *did* have "similar" feelings for Sandy, assuming she loved him as a brother. Guilt rapped him on the knuckles. He was playing semantics with a dying woman. If he were totally honest with himself, he would have to admit he had no idea how Sandy felt about him. They'd known each other for years, ever since he entered the seminary, and he'd always considered her a close friend—like a sister.

Was it possible she had told her mother something different?

"Before I die, my dearest wish is to see Sandy settled down in a good marriage. And I can think of no one more suitable for her than you are, Pastor Brad." She directed her sharp, clear eyes at him. No addle-brained dying woman speaking here. She knew exactly what she was after.

He shifted in his chair, trying to figure out what his next words should be. Mrs. Davey reached over and tried to give his hand an encouraging squeeze, but the weak grip almost broke his heart. How could he not grant a dying woman her last wish? It was in his power, but was it right to promise something he knew he wouldn't deliver?

He decided it wasn't.

"You know, Mrs. Davey," he began, choosing his words with care. "Sandy and I have never discussed marriage. We're very fond of each other, as you have observed, but the word marriage has never come up."

She was looking up at him, eyes filled with hope.

He cringed inside, hesitating, but then went on. "Of course no one can predict what the future will bring." The next thing he knew, he'd stepped right into it. He knew he should have avoided it, but couldn't help it. "And who knows if one day Sandy and I will tie the knot."

"If I could be assured of that, I would die in peace, a most happy woman and mother," Mrs. Davey whispered. "I would dearly love to see a ring on Sandy's finger before I die."

This was blackmail. Brad's high regard for the woman took a nosedive and he tried to hide his resentment from her scrutinizing eyes.

"Well, that's ... um, that's—" How did one respond to blackmail in a non-offensive way?

"I'm not trying to coerce you into anything, Pastor Brad, if that's what you're thinking."

That was *exactly* what he was thinking. Brad shrunk away from her in dismay. Was this weak, dying woman stronger than he'd suspected? Just how much had she dominated Sandy's life and steered her decision-making? He knew Sandy wasn't an assertive type, but this mother of hers seemed to possess enough backbone for the two of them.

"I understand your concern, Mrs. Davey," he replied, keeping his voice firm. Her audacity helped him to steel himself. "But I won't know if Sandy even wants to get married to me until I speak to her."

Mrs. Davey smiled and sighed with deep satisfaction—at least that's how it seemed to him. She closed her eyes briefly, and when she opened them Brad could almost see the steel in the gray irises.

"You don't have to worry about that, Pastor Brad. I have already spoken to Sandy and she assures me she loves you dearly and looks forward to your marriage."

Brad's hair stood on end. He had no intention of ever getting involved with any woman—not after what he'd done to Ann. He was through playing with women's feelings, and had been for years, but now it looked like he was being shanghaied into a marriage against his will by a dying woman. He was disappointed with Sandy, whom he'd trusted and considered his best friend.

"Well, in that case, I'll certainly speak to Sandy."

He rose and with a brief good-bye, he escaped out of the room.

Lord, help him, how was he going to get out of this?

Katharine and Maggie sat in the fifth row, which had become their "customary pew". Maggie raised her hand high and waved to Brad when she caught his eye, causing a few uplifted eyebrows.

Katharine gave her a gentle nudge with her elbow. "You greet Pastor Scott *after* the service," she whispered. "You don't see anybody else waving to him, do you?"

"I just wanted to say hi."

"You say hi *after* the service."

"Okay, okay. You don't have to get mad," Maggie hissed back, obviously offended. "How would I know how every little thing is done around here?"

Poor baby. Of course she didn't know. Katharine placed a placating hand on her daughter's arm, but Maggie was too indignant to respond. Still she let it lie there.

The organ began to grandly grind out a hymn, one of Katharine's favorites from her youth. She smiled at Maggie's enthusiasm as the girl listened, enthralled, forgetting to remain angry. Maggie read the words from the hymnal and by the third verse her clear, child's soprano joined in the melody.

Today, during the opening hymn and liturgy, Brad didn't even glance in their direction. Then, when he began the sermon, Katharine waited for him to turn and look their way. He didn't. Not once in the twenty minutes did his eyes waver from their focus on the text, except when he briefly raised his head to survey the choir loft and the right side of the church. Only the right side.

Why was he ignoring them?

Brad chanted the mantra in his head as he recited the lines of the liturgy by rote. *I will* not *look at her. I will* not *look at her.* He didn't want to make a fool of himself as he had the other Sunday when, distracted by the intense gaze from those incredible eyes, he'd lost his place.

Suddenly, to his dismay, the text of the sermon blurred before him. A pair of aquamarine eyes looked up at him from the page.

"Let us pray," he quickly said, and closed the book.

He bowed his head. He could not—must not—allow himself to be enchanted by this woman, not after what he'd done to Ann. He'd made a promise to God. Amen.

As the congregation sang the next hymn, he sat on the side bench and looked up at the choir loft again. There was Sandy giving him her usual wink and bright smile.

What was on her mind? Was it really possible Sandy had planned something with her mother? Was Sandy really in love with him? Well, she'd never given him any reason to think she was. He knew this with absolute certainty because—he smirked ironically at the altar flowers—when one considered all the years he'd dallied around with women, he could never have missed the signals, had there been any.

Or then he'd totally lost his touch.

Brad felt resentment grow inside him at the prospect of having to speak to Sandy about the marriage. The thought that Mrs. Davey—and maybe even Sandy—had put him in this uncomfortable position was grating.

He also resented the fact that he had to keep his eyes from straying toward Katharine. That, of course, was no one's fault but his own. Yet he *wanted* to look at her. He *loved* looking at her. But he couldn't allow himself to love any woman after throwing Ann's love back in her face in such a callous manner.

And with such horrible consequences.

Last week it had become very obvious he was in danger of becoming infatuated with Katharine. Sitting there in her apartment, being so near to her, and looking into those beguiling eyes of hers—that spelled danger. In the future he must avoid putting himself into such situations.

Except that every Sunday he would be greeting her at the door and holding her hand for a few seconds. It was no use telling himself the contact didn't give him pleasure, and it was getting difficult to resist the strong pull she had on him. He wanted to be with her. He wanted to take her in his arms and kiss those full lips.

Brad started as the closing hymn finished. He could feel the congregation shuffle as they waited for him to rise and give the final blessing.

After the final Amen he walked to the door to greet the people almost in a daze. And before he was ready for them, Katharine and Maggie were standing in front of him.

"Hello, Maggie. Hello, Mrs. Wilder." He looked at Katharine, then, because he had to. Pain slashed through his heart. He wished he could just give himself the freedom to love her. There was something about Katharine that told him it would be wonderful to have her love him in return.

Despite his most valiant attempts not to think about her, he'd ended up doing just that, every day and every night. It reminded him of the "White Bear Experiment" he'd learned about in psychology class, in which people were told not to think about a white bear, and that's exactly what they'd all ended up thinking about.

Katharine. Katharine. His white bear, whom he couldn't stop thinking about. Since she came into his life he'd spent countless hours—useless hours—trying to keep her face from appearing before him, especially when he'd lain awake at night tossing and turning in his bed.

Now, when the people filed down to the assembly hall for refreshments, Brad was drawn, whether he wanted to or not, into joining Katharine and Maggie at their table. Soon he and Maggie were immersed in a spirited conversation about the activities of the Youth Group. Although Katharine remained on the sidelines, listening, his body responded to her presence in ways he didn't want to acknowledge.

"Mrs. Wilder," Brad said when Maggie had stopped chattering for a moment, her mouth full of cake. "I was happy to hear Cantor Jones tell me you have joined the choir. I hope you'll find it rewarding and enjoyable."

"I'm sure I will, Pastor Scott," Katharine said. "I used to sing in my high school choir and I'm looking forward to next Thursday."

Brad looked at his watch. "If you'll excuse me, I have to get back upstairs to do a baptism." He rose. "Thank you for letting me share your table." He dared to look directly at Katharine and, as he'd feared, he found himself almost drowning in the aquamarine depths of her eyes. God, if she only knew how she affected him.

He turned to Maggie. "I'll see you Tuesday night?"

"Right on," Maggie said, and gave him a thumbs up.

After picking Maggie up from Youth Group, Katharine listened while the girl bubbled with anecdotes of the evening's activities. Sandy had been there again to help out Brad, and she was "like totally so nice."

"Sandy and Pastor Brad laughed and joked around together like a couple of teenagers." And Maggie went on to tell in great detail about all the funny things the two had said and done.

Katharine would much rather not have listened, but she had no choice.

"You know, Mom, I think they're just made for each other." Maggie sighed as she stretched, and then snuggled down into the seat. "They really are a pair. And personally," Maggie went on in an important voice, "I think Sandy's like totally in love with Pastor Brad. And I believe there *will* be an engagement, even if Pastor Brad said no."

"And is he like totally in love with her, too?" Katharine couldn't help the sarcastic edge in her voice.

Maggie tossed her disdainful glance. "Of *course* he is."

"And how have you come to that conclusion?"

"Because they're so perfect for each other. That's why. I think without her he'd be pretty lonely," Maggie mused. "Nobody around to have fun with. Kind of like when you and Daddy aren't married any more, you get lonely. Daddy's got Madeline, but you don't have nobody."

Katharine was thankful the evening shadows hid her shocked face. How had Maggie figured that one out? "I don't have anybody," she robotically corrected her daughter.

"Yeah, I know, Mom." Maggie patted her mother's arm. "And I think you should. You need a man to come home to."

Katharine suppressed a smile. Yes, and for other reasons, too. Aloud she said, "And to help with all the problems life throws at us."

Maggie squirmed beside her. "Like dealing with kids who do stupid things?"

"Among other things." Katharine stopped the car at a red light.

"Yeah." Maggie acknowledged her misdeed with a deep sigh. "I know."

As the light turned green and they moved on, Maggie nestled as close to Katharine as her seatbelt would allow. She rubbed her cheek against her mother's shoulder that, Katharine knew, meant Maggie wanted something. It was an old ploy with an amazing success rate.

"What is it now, Munchkin?" Katharine asked, reaching over to rumple Maggie's hair. "You have something up your sleeve, I can tell."

"Well, you know how they announced in church that they're going this weekend on a day-trip to their summer camp in Muskoka?" Maggie purred. "Do you think we could go, too? Huh, Mumsy-bumsy?"

"Stop calling me Mumsy-bumsy."

Maggie knew not to take the rebuke seriously. "Mumsy-bumsy-wumsy-dear, can we go too?"

Katharine smiled. "Well, maybe—."

Maggie jiggled under her seatbelt. "Pastor Brad told us they're going early Saturday morning and coming back later in the afternoon. So can we go, too?"

Katharine wanted to give in, just to see her daughter's face beam with joy, but she made one last attempt at stalling the inevitable. "I was going to plan some activities for the sand and water table this weekend," she began weakly. "I really—"

"Mom, *I'll* brain-storm with you. I've got dozens of

great ideas for sand and water. You know how I love mud."

"I wasn't thinking of mud."

"Same diff. And I'll probably think up a dozen more ideas while I'm on the beach. Pretty please, Mom?"

"It's too cold to swim."

"We'll just have fun on the beach."

By the time they entered the underground parking, Katharine had given in. They didn't get out of the city and into the country nearly often enough.

When triumphant Maggie was finally settled in bed, Katharine sat at the kitchen table to do her homework. But instead of making her plans, she tried to visualize a whole day being near Brad. Maybe she would have a chance to find out more about him, and why he was snubbing her, because she was sure that's what he was doing.

Maybe it had to do with Sandy, after all. Maybe there was a possibility the two of them were planning to get married, despite his firm denial. She wanted to find out, before she spent any more emotional capital on the man.

Unfortunately she would have to bring along her schoolwork and withdraw to some secluded place to work, but she could try to have enough contact with Brad to sort things out. She hoped.

Chapter Seven

After an absence of too many years, Katharine looked forward to singing in a choir again, even if there would be little likelihood of seeing Brad at the rehearsals. After all, what reason would he have to come to listen to a choir practice, for goodness sake? Still, even if singing wouldn't take her closer to her goal, she was keen to go.

She entered the church by the little side door and walked into the downstairs foyer. Many people had already arrived and friendly chatter filled the place. One of the women she'd met earlier in church took Katharine under her wing and introduced her to the others.

Of course Sandy was there, and to her dismay Katharine had to admit Maggie and Mrs. Ericson were right. What a sunny little woman Sandy was! Although Katharine tried to dismiss her as just another tiny, cute, curly-haired blonde, she couldn't fail to note Saint Sandy seemed to almost radiate goodness.

Angry with herself for her uncharitable thoughts, Katharine joined the alto section up on the choir loft. They were rehearsing two hymns for the next service, and she struggled to follow the unfamiliar notes and words, while at the same time keeping an eye on Cantor Jones. Not having sung in a choir since her high school days, she at first found sight-reading a challenge, and decided she'd have to take the sheet music home and brush up on the alto part before Sunday.

Although she had an ulterior motive for joining the choir, Katharine found herself enjoying the experience more than she'd imagined. Luckily she hadn't forgotten the rules of breath control and diction that had been drummed into her by her high school music teacher.

She was so busy focusing on the sheet music, it wasn't until she looked up from the notes, that she saw Brad standing there, resting his elbows on the piano.

"Well, Pastor Brad, to what do we owe this unexpected visit?" Cantor Jones asked when the song was over. The singers called out their greetings to him and he saluted them collectively with a smile and a small wave of his hand.

"I was looking over some papers in the office and heard this awful yowling, so I thought I'd better come and see if some poor animal was caught in the doors or something."

When the laughter had died down he said, "Actually you sound better than ever."

"Must be the newest addition to our ranks." Cantor Jones beamed. "Mrs. Wilder has joined the altos."

"Yes, so you told me," Brad remarked, pulling up a chair. "I think I'll stick around and listen some more." He seated himself astride facing the singers, and leaned his chin on his fists on the back of the chair. The outline of his muscular shoulders showed prominently through the light cotton shirt and Katharine found it difficult to draw her eyes away from him. How was she supposed to concentrate on her music with him sitting there, right in front of her eyes?

They began to rehearse the second hymn. It was one Katharine knew from her high school days, so she was able to sing with more freedom and enjoy the way her low alto voice blended with the others.

But in the middle of the song, she glanced at Brad over the notes and saw him wink at someone in the soprano section. Sandy? Katharine strove to fix her attention firmly on Cantor Jones's waving arms and to keep her eyes on the dancing black dots before her.

After a while she couldn't prevent her eyes from wandering back to Brad—for just one more stolen glance. To her surprise and pleasure she found him looking right at her, but when their eyes met, his gaze immediately shifted away. Shaken to the core, Katharine again struggled to find her place in the hymnal. Then, when she looked up again, Brad was gone. Disappointment mixed with relief filled her in a most confusing way. Good. He was gone and now she could concentrate on her singing again. But, perversely, she also wanted to have him sitting there, so she could take the occasional peek at him and his dark blue eyes.

Katharine thought he'd left for the evening, but when break-time came and everyone went downstairs into the kitchen, there was Brad, helping himself to a mug of coffee and a biscuit. He sat down at a table with a few friends.

"Come and sit with us, Mrs. Wilder," he called to her.

Katharine's heart did a joyful somersault. Carrying her coffee and a cookie, she walked over and seated herself beside John Hopkins, who had spoken to her earlier. She smiled at him. "How is it going over there in the tenor section?"

"Could be better," John Hopkins replied with a rueful laugh. "We need some younger singers who can reach those darned high notes. Too bad you aren't a man, Mrs. Wilder."

"Oh, but we wouldn't want that," Brad exclaimed and drew laughter from everyone around the table. "I mean the altos are really happy to have her," he added, looking a bit flustered.

"I can certainly agree with Pastor Brad that we're happy to have this lovely addition to the choir *and* to the congregation," John said, nodding gallantly at Katharine.

"Thank you kindly, Mr. Hopkins, sir," Katharine said in a southern drawl, eliciting more laughter.

At last it looked like things were beginning to click. Brad had actually complimented her. Feeling happy with the way things were developing, Katharine sat back and didn't hear much of the conversation after that.

The rehearsal continued and with no Brad to distract her, Katharine sang like she hadn't done in years. Following the able direction of Cantor Jones, she took pride in quickly learning her cues. She sang the notes with increasing confidence and pleasure, for there was something about the peaceful harmony of the hymns that soothed her and freed her for a moment from all her worries.

Afterwards, as everyone was preparing to leave, Brad came back to say good night to everyone, without a special word to Katharine. Then, laughing and joking with Sandy, they walked out together with his arm around her shoulders.

Damn! So much for things clicking.

The forecast for Saturday promised a beautiful day, but the conditions in Katharine's heart weren't as sunny. Since the choir practice she'd been regretting she ever agreed to come. At first she'd hoped this outing would give her a chance to figure out why Brad seemed to be avoiding her, but if he and Sandy were a "pair", then it was a moot point and there was nothing for her to figure out. As for his so-called "compliment" at the choir practice, when she thought about it in the cold light of day, it had really been nothing more than part of the silly chatter around the table.

Since all hope of him being attracted to her was doomed, it annoyed her that, try as she might, she still couldn't get the man out of her mind. She was wasting her time kicking a dead horse, for God's sake. She had to face facts. Even if tiny sparkling Sandy hadn't been lurking in the background, he probably wouldn't have been interested in someone like Katharine. She was tall and husky. Once a man had even called her Junoesque, but luckily he'd meant it as a compliment. That so-called "spark of interest and admiration" she'd hung all her hopes on was probably nothing more than a bout of indigestion brought on by too many doughnuts.

When she'd called up the church to ask about the Saturday outing, she'd been relieved it was Mrs. Ericson, not Brad, who picked up the phone. It was much easier to speak about pies and sandwiches when she didn't also have to deal with a fluttering heart and wobbling vocal cords. Katharine had promised to bring a couple of apple pies, and Mrs. Ericson had thanked her so profusely it sounded suspiciously like no one else was bringing anything.

Following the directions she'd received from Mrs. Ericson, Katharine and Maggie proceeded north to Muskoka. The sight of bare bedrock that had been scraped smooth by glaciers, plunging deep into dazzling blue waters, never failed to stir Katharine's romantic soul. Today, however, she was almost oblivious to the rough, barren beauty, which saved Maggie from a lecture on The Group of Seven artists. Instead Katharine gripped the steering wheel and stared mutely at the road. What a fun outing this was going to be.

She didn't want to arrive, but too soon they were at Pine Lake, and she circled into the parking lot of the Redemption Church Muskoka Retreat. Maggie jumped out immediately and ran off, eager to find her friends, while Katharine gathered the piles of schoolwork from the back seat into her arms. Holding the shield of books and papers against her chest, she walked toward the long, rustic log building standing on a small knoll, not far from the sandy shore. A verandah circled around the three sides overlooking the lake.

Katharine opened the wide wooden door and entered, looking around the large room for somewhere to place her books. The walls were of horizontal light pine logs, and the wide floorboards, wearing dents from heavy use, looked like they'd been scrubbed clean. Long wooden tables, covered with white wax cloth, took up the space along the walls, but the middle of the room had been left open, Katharine assumed, for activities. To the right, a door opened into the kitchen, from where emanated a cacophony of female voices and the delicious aroma of food. It looked like her apple pies wouldn't be the only item on the menu after all.

Katharine laid her books on one of the tables and peeked into the kitchen. Mrs. Ericson saw her and immediately came over, wiping her hands on her large white apron.

"I am so glad you found us, dear. I was afraid my directions weren't clear enough." She led Katharine into the kitchen and introduced her to the other three ladies.

Brad was nowhere to be seen, and Katharine hoped she could just work in peace and not have to meet him at all. All her plans for trying to find out why he was avoiding her had flown out the window and it was now *she* who wanted to avoid *him*. So much for throwing her hat in the ring. She didn't have to experience a knockout before conceding defeat. Since her feelings weren't going to be reciprocated, she wasn't about to waste her emotional energy on him, and thus wouldn't even give him a passing thought all day.

As if that was going to be possible.

"I'll get the pies from the car," she told Mrs. Ericson. "I'm afraid I'm going to have to find a quiet spot to do some schoolwork. I hate to be unsociable, but it's absolutely necessary I get some planning done. I just brought Maggie here because she wanted so badly to come."

"Of course, dear. I understand," Mrs. Ericson said. "There's an office right over there, where you won't be disturbed."

When Katharine had deposited the pies in the kitchen, she picked up her books and followed Mrs. Ericson across the dining hall to a door that led into a cozy little room.

"This is Pastor Brad's office, but I'm sure you won't be disturbed," Mrs. Ericson assured her. "I won't even tell anyone you're here, except Maggie, of course."

Along one wall of the office was a low bookshelf, filled to the brim with manuals, hymnals, and religious texts. Sitting at the large desk in front of the window would give Katharine a fabulous view of the sandy beach, the sparkling blue lake, and some small, rocky islands in the distance.

"This is perfect," she said, delighted. "I can look out the window and not feel like I'm missing everything. Thank you so much."

Mrs. Ericson turned to go. "I'll bring you a cup of coffee and a cookie or two. And whenever you need anything, just come into the kitchen and ask. Lunch will be around twelve-thirty."

With the steaming coffee in front of her, Katharine tried to settle down to work. The little office was quite warm, and after a while, with the door closed, it started to feel stuffy. Katharine removed her sweatshirt and pants. Underneath she was wearing a sleeveless tee shirt and shorts, because the weatherman on TV had said there was the possibility of reaching record highs today. She ran her palms over her smooth, long legs. Some tan would make them look better.

Katharine turned to her work. Sand and water ... sand and water. The blank paper stared back at her. What could the children do with sand and water in the classroom without creating a flood? Or mud.

Outside the lake glittered with dancing diamonds and the sandy beach had attracted about two dozen kids. They were prancing around in shorts and tee shirts, and she longed to join them in the warm sunshine.

It looked like a race was going on to see which group could build the biggest sand castle and, of course, Maggie was right there in the thick of things. A shrinking violet she definitely was not, and Katharine was glad of that, remembering her own difficulties as an only child. How often she'd wished for a sister who would be a companion to her in new situations. Maybe she wasn't such a bad mother, after all, seeing as how Maggie had turned out to be such a confident young person. But then this confident young person had hitched up with the wrong kind of friends and ended up at the police station. Of course she wasn't chumming around with them anymore, but still, maybe it wasn't quite the time to pat herself on the back.

Katharine sighed and tried to bring her mind back to the work in front of her. Sand and water.

There was Sandy, kneeling in the sand, looking like just one of the kids, laughing and shoveling, her blonde curls bobbing as she dug enthusiastically. When she bent forward, her little behind looked young and firm in her shorts. She was probably only in her mid-twenties.

Wouldn't any man be happier with a more experienced woman? Like Katharine? She turned to look at herself in the mirror above the low bookshelf. Her wide brow and high cheekbones made her look more mature than her thirty-plus years, but her graceful, long neck softened that appearance. Of course her strong jaw always made her seem determined and purposeful, but—she raised her chin—that's what she was. In fact, if she wanted to, she could take Brad away from Sandy with the flick of her little finger. If only he were interested in her. So much for maturity and determination.

She turned to her work again and noted with dismay the paper was still as blank as it had been half an hour ago. To make it seem like she had accomplished something, she wrote "Sand and Water Activities" at the top. After ten minutes, when no ideas had surfaced, she rose to go to the kitchen to refill her empty coffee mug.

Before she reached the door, it opened and Brad stepped in. He stopped just inside the room, and his eyes flew open in surprise. For a moment they stood, facing each other, neither knowing what to say. Katharine's racing heart pumped color to her cheeks.

"Hello, Pastor Scott," she finally blurted out, feeling like a child caught in a naughty act. "I'm just ... Mrs. Ericson told me I could work here."

"Of course." Brad looked almost as flustered as she felt. "No problem. I just didn't know you were in here. I'm sorry I disturbed your work." The door of the room began to slowly swing shut on its own and Brad reached out behind him to kick it open with his foot.

"I was just ... just going to the kitchen for a refill," Katharine said, holding out her empty cup as evidence, while trying to compose herself. "You didn't disturb anything." Why was she so agitated? Like this was the first time she'd ever been alone with a man.

The door began to close again, and once more he pushed it open, but remained there, blocking the way, while she kept her eyes on her coffee cup, not daring to look up at him.

She'd always considered herself tall for a woman, but the top of her head only reached his nose. Still flustered, she reached up to flick her dark auburn curls, which today she had unchained from the up-do that normally bound them, allowing the long strands to fall on her neck and shoulders. As she ran her fingers through the released locks, a little flirty devil entered her and liberated her from the constricting roles of mother and school teacher. Capriciously she tossed her head and threw a bold, silent challenge up to him. She saw his eyes flash darkly, the pupils dilating, and there was no question in her mind he *definitely* was into her.

"Katharine," Brad began, and then quickly amended, "Mrs. Wilder, you are looking quite—" He cleared his throat. "—quite well today."

She smiled. So a pair of shorts and a rather revealing top made her look well, did they? She should have left it with a simple thank you, but the flirty little devil made her grin playfully. "Thank you, Pastor Scott. You're looking quite well yourself. Less like a pastor and more like a man."

It was his hair. That sandy forelock tumbling rakishly over one eye. It was almost impossible to resist the impulse to raise her hand to brush it aside.

It was his turn to blush. He grinned self-consciously and raked the strands off his forehead.

How she loved that boyish gesture, and seeing it made her want to resume her efforts to connect with him. His reaction just now made her feel maybe this relationship had a future, after all. Yet, why did he always seem to withdraw just when she thought things were coming together? How *should* she approach him? Should she boldly show her interest or would that scare him off? Her natural inclination was to shoot-from-the-hip, but this was too important to mess up.

Katharine decided to play it safe.

"I'm getting some coffee," she said and started to brush past him. But this time, when the door started to close behind him, he didn't push it open. The room shrunk in size as the walls enclosed them into a little private space. Her heart pounded and the sudden rush of blood into her head made her dizzy. She was standing so close to him, he had to see the pulse hammering at her throat.

Brad's hand came up and touched her hair. "Beautiful," he murmured.

Katharine's heart did a flip. How should she respond to this intimate gesture? The natural temptation was to turn toward him and show him very clearly how this affected her. That would push the relationship very quickly into new territory. Was this what he intended by his gesture?

All this went through her mind in a flash as she stood almost against his chest. What should she do? Panic filled her, and she pushed past him, flinging open the door. She almost flew into the dining hall where a woman wiping the tables looked up, surprised at her sudden appearance. With a quick nod, Katharine marched past her into the kitchen.

She filled her cup and remained there, chatting with the ladies long enough to calm herself before venturing outside. She stood on the verandah that encircled the building and took in several deep breaths. What a coward she was! What an opportunity lost. Or was it? What if Brad's gesture was simply brought on by a sudden impulse, and he had no intention of having it lead to anything more? In that case she'd acted in a perfectly appropriate manner.

Schoolwork was now out of the question. Katharine wandered down to the beach, where Maggie interrupted her shoveling long enough to wave. Katharine walked over to each group and, like the teacher she was, made favorable comments on the size and shape of each sand castle.

Sandy laughed and stood up. She wiped her face with the back of her hand, leaving a smudge of wet sand on her nose. "I think we'll have to go for a swim even if the water's still freezing cold," she said. "They won't let us in for lunch, looking like this."

"For your sake I hope they will," Katharine replied. "Because the kitchen smells absolutely delicious and the water, as you said, is absolutely freezing."

The sand was warm and she bent down to remove her sandals. Out of the corner of her eye she saw the furtive glances of young male eyes eyeing her breasts, and wished she'd put the sweatshirt back on before coming out. Straightening up, she turned to go back to the house. Now if it had been Brad ogling her, she wouldn't have minded one bit.

Brad's bare toes dug into the soft sand as he sauntered down toward the beach. What an idiot he was. He wished he could dig himself a hole in the sand and disappear, preferably head first. Why on earth did he have to go and touch her hair, like some adoring schoolboy? The answer was simple. Because it had been impossible not to. She'd looked so different from the person he was used to seeing around the church. Today she looked exactly like the desirable, sexy woman he dreamt about every night.

He'd not had any difficulty—not till Katharine came into his life—of keeping away from women. At first he thought he could easily learn to ignore Katharine, just as he'd ignored all other women who'd made a play for him. But Katharine wasn't that easy to ignore. She drew him like a magnet. He could tell under that cloak of motherhood was a woman who was passionate. Desirable. Sexy. And what made it even more difficult was that she was sending him subtle but strong signals she was interested in starting a relationship.

So there he'd stood, simpering like a mindless idiot. God, why wasn't he struck mute before he had a chance to make a fool of himself? She probably dashed out of the room to save him the embarrassment of hearing her burst into gales of laughter. He could just imagine her standing around the corner of the building, trying to stop her giggling.

Then he saw her. She was coming straight toward

him and it was impossible to change direction without making it look like he was trying to avoid her. He had every intention of passing by with just a nod, but as they came face to face, he felt he had to say something.

He stopped, and then couldn't get a word out of his mouth.

Katharine also stopped. Standing in front of him, she was obviously waiting for him to speak. There was nothing to do but confront the situation.

"Mrs. Wilder, I'm sorry," he said. "I don't know what got into me in there."

She looked like she expected him to continue, so he did, wishing with each word he could just shut up. Or sink into the sand. "You just look so different today with your hair down, and dressed..." He swallowed and did his utmost not to look down at her ample bosom, but failed. "... like that."

"That's all right, pastor. Don't give it another thought," she replied, and he could see a little devil lurking in her eyes. "These things happen. I'll see you later." She slung her sandals over her shoulder and, with a swing of her hips, swept by him.

Brad, a man of the cloth, couldn't help cursing under his breath. She probably thought his experience with women was limited to stroking someone's hair. Where was the "love 'em and leave 'em Don Juan" of his previous life when the guy was needed? That confident and skillful manipulator of women. And baby-killer.

His previous life was over. The tragedy of it was that he'd caused Ann such horrible suffering before he'd learned his lesson. Katharine, at least, was safe from him.

He pasted a grin on his face before he reached the sand castle builders and bent down to join Sandy's team. A chorus of protesters stopped him.

"Pastor Brad, no fair you helping Sandy!" a girl yelled.

"I know she's your girlfriend and all, but our team needs help more than hers," Maggie piped up.

Brad glanced at Sandy, waiting for her to deny the relationship, but she only smiled and continued to dig. After the interview with Mrs. Davey, he couldn't help wondering what was on her mind. He'd have to have a talk with her at the earliest opportunity and find out what, exactly, was going on.

Chapter Eight

Katharine entered the office and again she tried to concentrate on the assignment, but the touch of Brad's hand on her hair and his whispered word didn't leave her in peace. They replayed in her brain like a broken record. She would have loved to believe his actions meant he was attracted to her, but, darn it all, Sandy was there, lurking on the sand. Katharine would only make a fool of herself if she came onto him when he seemed to be involved with someone else.

If she only knew for sure what was going on.

She stared blankly at the title on the page in front of her. This was so unfair. For years she'd dreamed of meeting someone like Brad—so perfect in every way for her *and* for Maggie. Someone who could make her heart beat the way Brad did whenever he was near. Closing her eyes, Katharine relived the secure and comforting grip of his hand and his gentle touch on her hair.

And now that she'd found him, it looked like his heart was already taken.

She sighed, picked up the pencil, and absently twirled it in her fingers. By the time Mrs. Ericson knocked on the door to announce that lunch was ready, not a single sand and water play activity had appeared on the paper.

Katharine joined Maggie at one of the long tables and apologized to Mrs. Ericson for not having helped with the preparations.

Her words were tut-tutted aside. "Don't even think about such things, my dear. There are plenty of people here to help out. You just enjoy your meal and go back to work, if you have to. But I hope you'll have a chance to go for a walk and take advantage of this beautiful day." Mrs. Ericson added.

Katharine nodded. "Yes, I was thinking I might do that after lunch."

With the meal over, Katharine strode toward a rocky, wooded hill. The terrain was mainly soft pine needles layered upon the bedrock and she marveled at the ability of the tall pines to get enough sustenance from such scant soil. She climbed higher and higher. Even with just her shorts and tee shirt on he was soon feeling quite warm. It was great to be young and nimble-footed—

Suddenly her foot slipped on some dry needles that covered the smooth, sloping rock face. With a cry of surprise she slid down and fell off a ledge and landed a few feet below with an excruciating jolt. For a moment she lay still, assessing where the pain was the greatest. Her left knee was bent under her in an agonizing twist. She tried to straighten it, but the sharp pain made her cry out.

Katharine looked around to assess the situation. She hadn't brought her cell phone with her, because she knew out here in the "wilderness of Muskoka" there was no reception. So now what? She'd fallen into a kind of crevasse, surrounded on one side by the rock from which she had tumbled, and on all other sides by shrubs, boulders and trees. What an awkward place to get out of.

She estimated she'd walked for about fifteen minutes when the accident happened, and was too far from the camp to be heard, if she called for help. No one would think of starting out to look for her for at least an hour or more, for she'd let them know she would be going on a fairly long hike. After her walk, she'd told them, she would return to the office to work. They would think she'd be there, and wouldn't want to disturb her.

Lying for an hour or more in the shadowy crevasse, on damp, dead leaves and pine needles, among bugs, spiders and who knew what else, was not an appealing option. So, unless she wanted to sit here for at least a couple of hours— probably more—she had to try to get back on her own.

She cursed her luck with a few choice expletives and then, holding her breath, began to force the injured leg out from under her. A moan escaped from between her gritted teeth, but once the leg was straight, she found the pain less severe. There didn't seem to be any broken bones from what she could determine, but she suspected the knee was badly sprained.

Grasping the lowest tree branches and shrubs for the slight support they could offer, she inched up to a standing position. As she pulled herself up the sloping rock face once again, beads of sweat streamed down her forehead and she grimaced with pain. With every breath she gasped, "You can do it, girl!"

Although her progress was extremely slow and painful, finally she was lying on her stomach at the top, drenched in perspiration. She knew it would be impossible to put any weight on the left leg, and hopping on one foot on that terrain was out of the question. If only she had a staff—but none of the trees around her had lower branches that looked sturdy enough. She had to resort to crawling on her hands and one knee, dragging the sprained leg behind her. Needles and jagged rocks scratched her hands and scraped her legs as she crept along the forest floor, while the injured knee throbbed with excruciating pain.

She had no idea how long it took her to reach the edge of the parking lot, but by then she was sobbing in agony and faint with fatigue. Her clothes were filthy and glued to her body with dirt and sweat. Every inch of bare skin had nasty, bleeding scratches. She sat up against a tree trunk and tried to call for help, but there was no one in sight. She heard laughter down by the beach, but her cries didn't carry that far.

Katharine closed her eyes.

Panic-stricken cries awakened her and she slit open her eyes just enough to see Sandy kneeling over her.

"Brad! Brad!" Sandy called. "Come quickly! Something has happened to Katharine."

And the next thing Katharine felt were Brad's arms gently lifting her, holding her against his chest, and carrying her toward the main building. She grimaced and cried in pain each time her knee jolted.

"It'll be all right, darling," Brad whispered against her hair, comforting her like he would a child. "It's all right. You're safe now."

Sandy and Mrs. Ericson followed close behind, with Maggie circling around them, almost tripping Brad in her concern. He carried Katharine into a small bedroom off the main area and laid her down on a bed. Through the haze of pain she was conscious of an irrational joy in her heart. Darling? Had he called her darling? Or had she just imagined it?

Everyone began to fuss over her. Brad withdrew, leaving the cleaning and dressing of her cuts to Sandy and Mrs. Ericson.

When Katharine was all bandaged up and changed into her sweats, she lay on the bed feeling quite comfortable, except for the throbbing in her left knee. Maggie, her face scrunched in a worried frown, pulled up a little wooden stool and sat beside Katharine, holding her hand.

Sandy went to get Brad, who sat down at the foot of the bed and looked at Katharine with concern. "Are you in great pain?" he asked.

"Only when I laugh," she managed to quip.

"Mom," Maggie said severely. "Be serious. This isn't funny."

Katharine gave her a rueful smile. "You're right, sweetie. The knee really does hurt if I even think about it."

"Should we call an ambulance to take you to the hospital in Rocky Harbor?" Brad asked. "Or can you manage to sit in a car while I drive?"

"I think I can sit in a car without too much discomfort." Actually, there probably would be quite a lot of discomfort, but Katharine was ready to grit her teeth and not be a difficult patient.

"I assume we'll be at the hospital for quite a while," Brad said. "So Mrs. Ericson and Sandy will stay here and take care of things. I thought maybe Sandy could take Maggie home after the camp is over?" He looked at Maggie, who nodded her consent. "And Sandy could stay with you till I bring your mother home?"

Maggie nodded again. "Yeah. That's okay with me."

Brad turned back to Katharine. "Maybe Sandy could drive your car back? She came here with me."

"That sounds like a plan," Katharine agreed. "I just wish I weren't messing up this whole day for everyone."

"Don't you worry none about that," Mrs. Ericson said. "These things happen and we just have to deal with them. We can thank God you didn't break your neck, falling like that."

"You can lie down in the back of the car, Mom." Maggie stroked her mother's cheek. "Because you can't sit with your leg sticking out."

Katharine's heart was giving almost visible leaps of joy. It looked like her brain had gone AWOL and her loudly hammering heart had taken over. Forget Sandy. Brad was going to be hers for a few hours.

So much for her determination to avoid him.

As Brad carried Katharine to the parking lot, Katharine wrapped her arms around his neck, ostensibly to lighten the load, but actually determined to relish every moment of closeness. Being carried by him was infinitely nicer than just having him shake her hand.

Everyone buzzed around, helping her into the back seat of Brad's car, and Katharine tried not to cry out.

Maggie planted a final kiss on her mother's cheek. "Just take it easy, Mom. I'll take care of you when you get home."

"I know you will, sweetie. I'll be all right."

Katharine could tell Brad was trying to drive as smoothly as possible, avoiding the ruts on the country road. Unfortunately this wasn't always successful, and Brad kept apologizing whenever she gasped with pain as they hit a pothole. Finally they were coasting along the highway, and Katharine found sitting in the back, her knee supported by two pillows, wasn't too uncomfortable.

At first they drove in silence. It was as though they were both thinking of some safe, neutral subject with which to begin. Brad glanced in the rearview mirror from time to time, not only to check for traffic, but also to check up on her.

Finally Katharine broke the silence. She didn't want these precious moments with him to be wasted.

"Are you looking forward to conducting the summer camp in August?" she asked. That subject stood on pretty solid ground.

"Yes, I think I'll enjoy it," he replied.

"I was thinking that with a group of teenagers it might be quite challenging."

"It can be. The idea is that in between the swimming and sports and other activities we can help these young people learn to deal with some of the challenges they'll be facing in life."

"Good," Katharine agreed. "Because that's the reason I enrolled Maggie in your Youth Group. I was worried about the company she was keeping, and I'm hoping you'll instill in her whatever moral teaching I've been unable to get across. Doesn't say much for my teaching skills, does it?"

"From what I've seen so far, I think Maggie's a great kid. But you indicated there was something you wished to tell me. We won't be at the hospital for a while yet, so if you feel up to it, I guess now's as good a time as any to talk about it."

Katharine related the incident at the police station. "Being a single parent sucks, as the kids would say," she concluded.

Brad smiled. "I hear you, but I think you've done a super job with Maggie. Of course, the older she gets, the more temptations life will bring, so it won't hurt her to know that God has her back all the way."

"That sounds very comforting, even for us older kids," Katharine said, although she thought Brad's reassuring arms around her would give her all the comfort she would ever need. "Is that the main message you want to get across to them?" Katharine asked.

Brad turned to glance back at her. "Yes. That God is love. And if they ask sincerely, they can trust they will be forgiven no matter what they've done."

"That's a great message," she said.

"Yes, if one can only believe it."

Katharine was surprised to see Brad's jaw stiffen. Was he angry about something she'd said? His eyes, when he again glanced at the rearview mirror, looked sad.

What had brought this on?

For a few minutes he drove on, neither one speaking. The silence was becoming awkward, so finally Katharine asked, "So you're all set for the summer camp?"

She was relieved to see the angry set of his mouth

break into a mischievous grin as he directed his eyes back at her.

"Well, as a matter of fact, we're always looking for volunteers. Are you, by any chance, looking for a summer job?"

"Well, I *am* off all summer." She hesitated. "And I'm not planning to take any courses this year—"

"Thanks, that's great," he said. "I'll put your name on the list."

Katharine laughed. "Whoa! I wasn't *seriously* thinking—"

"Please do. We need people like you, experienced in dealing with kids."

His entreating voice made it difficult to refuse. "Okay," she said at last. "As long as my knee is healed by then."

What a dizzying turn of events. Had she really just promised to spend two whole weeks shepherding a bunch of teenagers and, what's more, being close to Brad? That could be hell. Or heaven.

Katharine watched him through the rearview mirror, feeling totally confused. Today she'd seen proof, just as she'd suspected, that Brad *was* attracted to her. With all the talk about him and Sandy, she'd begun to doubt her feminine instincts. Now, however, she was certain the interest was there. Stroking her hair, calling her "darling" when he carried her in his arms, a man didn't do that to a woman he didn't care about.

Was it because he was already somehow committed to Sandy that he didn't want to get too close to Katharine? That would have made sense, except she couldn't believe a man like Brad would do and say such things behind Sandy's back. He was a *preacher,* for God's sake, so that didn't compute. It had to be something else.

So, again, Katharine decided she must get to the bottom of whatever was driving him.

Hat back in the ring!

Of course it was possible what he felt for her was nothing more than sexual attraction. Surely even ministers weren't immune to such things. That, however, was not what she wanted. She'd been looking for someone to be there for her as a partner in life. To help her with Maggie now, and to be with her "in her remaining years", as Bonnie had put it. Now that she'd met Brad, she knew it wasn't just *someone* she wanted, but him. Her eyes filled with tears, and she tried to wipe them away surreptitiously.

Brad caught the movement in the rear mirror and turned to look at her. "Is your knee giving you pain?" he asked, concern in his voice.

"No ... not really," she replied.

He reached back and gave her leg a light, reassuring stroke. "We'll be at the hospital in just a couple of minutes."

He pulled up to the only traffic light in Rocky Harbor.

"I'm fine. Really," she insisted.

"So what were those tears for then, or shouldn't I ask?" His voice was only slightly jovial.

"I wouldn't go there if I were you," she countered in the same light tone.

He laughed. "I can't help wondering if they were for a lost love."

"Well, they're for a lost something. Maybe my lost mobility?"

Brad gripped the steering wheel. Never in his wildest dreams had he intended to ask Katharine to come to the camp. So how had the invitation slipped out of his mouth? Maybe in his wildest dreams he'd *wished* it could happen, but he knew that actually having her there for two weeks would be inviting trouble. A wave of panic rose inside him. He hadn't meant to go there, but he had. He'd asked the woman he was trying to stay away from to be at the camp—close to him—for two weeks.

He just hadn't been able to stop himself, because he so much *wanted* her near. *Wanted* to be with her. Every particle of his body was crying out for her. But there was nothing he could do about that, and having her at the camp was definitely not going to help.

Maybe he should apply for that position at the Victoria Harbor church he'd read about. If he was accepted, he'd be safely away from her.

Coward! He had no right to slink away from this punishment that was being heaped on him. Loving Katharine but not being able to have her was exactly what he deserved after hurting Ann. He slammed his palm against the steering wheel, causing Katharine to look at him with a puzzled frown.

"Is something the matter?"

"No. Nothing at all. I just remembered something I should have looked after." Like what? Liar as well as a hypocrite. "It's not a problem. I can do it later."

He looked in the mirror at Katharine, semi-reclined in the back seat. Ever since he'd found her in his office, he'd been aware of her presence, even when she wasn't around. Even playing volleyball with the kids, he'd been thinking of her, and—to his team's despair— had missed a few easy shots.

Luckily Katharine had no idea how attractive he found her. She didn't know how he'd felt when he'd carried her, holding her against his chest. Though he'd whispered words to her he never intended to, he hoped she hadn't heard. Or if she had, wouldn't think they meant anything. Though they did. Heaven help him, they did.

His arms still remembered the curves of her body when he'd held her, and they wanted to hold her again. He ached to see her smile, and longed again for the incredibly heady feeling that filled him when he looked into her eyes. He was tired of trying to avoid her, and he knew if he let himself love her, he'd be the happiest man on earth. How he wanted to grasp that happiness with both hands and tuck it deep in his heart.

But he knew that was impossible.

Brad turned into the hospital parking lot and stopped the car in front of the emergency doors.

"Speaking of mobility, do you have crutches at home, by any chance?" he asked.

"Oh, yes," she said, laughing. "I always keep some around, just in case."

"No, seriously. You're going to need them to get around for a while. We can get you a pair here, at the hospital."

When Katharine tried unsuccessfully to struggle out of the car, Brad couldn't help commenting, "See? I'm right. It's crutches for you. You're totally helpless, my dear. I'll go get us a wheelchair."

Brad went into the hospital and returned with an intern who helped deposit Katharine into a wheelchair. In the small waiting room they settled down for a long wait, but were surprised when just an hour later a doctor was free to look at her knee.

Brad wheeled her down the hall into an examination room. "There's something to be said for small-town hospitals. If we were in the city, we'd be here till midnight."

By the time she'd had an X-ray, had received a brace, and had been taught how to use her crutches, it was long past dinnertime.

"How about we stop for a quick take-out meal?" Brad suggested. That would give him more time to spend with her.

Katharine had kept Maggie informed of the situation by phone, and now called her again to tell her they would be late

"Looks like she and Sandy are all set," she told him. "They've already had dinner and are going to watch a DVD. They've even got some nachos and dip. Looks like I'm not missed one bit."

To make it easier on Katharine, they decided not to go to a restaurant and instead ate hamburgers in the car. Katharine sat in the back with her leg up, and Brad was in the front, his arm slung over the backrest, so he could see her more easily.

"What's the matter?" Katharine asked after a while. "Do I have mustard on my chin? You keep looking at me."

He started, not realizing he'd been staring. "No. I just can't get over the difference in your appearance when your hair is down like that." He stopped and then laughed to hide his embarrassment.

"Why, thank you, if by different you mean something complimentary," Katharine said, her voice deliberately coy.

Brad took a bite of his burger, but almost choked on it when she asked, "So is that why you called me darling? Because I looked nice?"

He flinched and could feel his ears burn. "Wh... what do you mean?" he stammered.

Katharine was obviously taken aback by his words for the blood rushed to her cheeks. This had to be embarrassing for her, but no more so than for him.

"When you were carrying me from the forest?" she reminded him in a small voice.

Still he said nothing. He couldn't. His throat was constricted by unchewed food.

"I probably heard you wrong. I'm sorry. I wasn't exactly in the greatest condition at the time, and I'm sure I just imagined the whole thing. There were so many people milling around and so much loud chatter—" Katharine was carrying on, looking as uncomfortable as he felt.

Brad finally swallowed his food. "No, you heard right," he owned up. "I didn't think you heard me. It just slipped out. You were so helpless and looked almost unconscious." He smiled then, and tried to put a humorous twist on the incident. "Actually I was just trying to distract you because at that point you looked like some kind of wounded forest troll."

She laughed at that. "I'm sure I looked even worse, all scratched up and covered in moss, with dead leaves in my hair and spiders and other horrid creepy-crawlies clinging to me." She shuddered.

Brad chuckled and the pressure was lifted. "Yes, you did look a bit scary."

They finished the meal in easy conversation about the summer camp as the evening shadows were lengthening.

After helping Katharine up to her condo, he drove home, surprised by the unexpected feeling of lightness in his heart. It was so strange he almost couldn't recognize it for what it was. Happiness. From having spent time with *her*.

And thoughts of Sandy and her mother hadn't popped up once the whole time.

Yes, that whole Sandy-affair was something he'd have to deal with right away. How, exactly, *did* things stand between them? He knew he only loved her as a dear friend, but what if Sandy loved him, as Mrs. Davey had told him, as a future husband, and was expecting him to propose?

What a mess!

Before he'd reached the parsonage, the feeling of lightness and happiness had all but evaporated.

It was time to face the music.

Brad sweated bullets while thinking how he would approach Sandy. He went over several possible versions of the scenario, from being totally blunt, to somehow getting her to reveal whether she loved him or not. And he desperately hoped it was "not".

As it turned out, it was easier than he could have hoped for.

After the young people had left on Tuesday evening,

Brad and Sandy stayed behind to put some finishing touches on the kitchen. The kids had cleared away the snacks and dishes, but there was always some rinsing and wiping up to do.

Brad draped the dishtowel over the oven door handle and decided this was as good a time as any to bite the bullet.

"I went to see your mother," he began. "She's not doing too well."

Sandy sighed and turned to face him. "No, she isn't." Her eyes misted.

"I'm sorry." He reached out to stroke her shoulder. "It's very hard on you."

She brushed away a tear. "I know she's not going to last much longer. The doctor says it's just a matter of maybe two or three months—maybe just a few weeks."

No avoiding it now. "So, maybe this is the worst possible time to bring this up, when things are so painful for you, but I have to know—" Brad swallowed. "Your mother asked me something, and it's been troubling me the last few days." Troubling wasn't half of it.

"Yes?"

They were leaning against the kitchen counter side by side, not facing each other, which made it easier for Brad to blurt out the words. "She asked me to look after you when she's gone. In fact she kind of intimated you and I should—"

Laughter was the last thing he expected to hear from Sandy. It took him completely off guard.

"I'm really sorry, Brad." Sandy wiped away her tears, which were there only partly from laughing. "Mom's so worried about me. She thinks I'm still a little girl, incapable of looking after myself, and for weeks she's been telling me if you and I got married, then you'd be there to look after me. Is that what she said to you, too?"

"Pretty much." Thank goodness! It didn't sound like Sandy and her mother were on the same page. "It's not that I'd be *unwilling* to look after you and help you out. But —"

Sandy put a hand on his arm. "Please, Brad," she said, still smiling. "You don't have to explain. I know you'd be willing to help, but I don't need anyone to look after me. After Mom is gone—" she stopped and the smile disappeared. Her chin trembled and again her eyes welled with tears. "After she's gone and all her affairs are in order, I'll be leaving."

"Leaving?"

Sandy nodded firmly. "That's right." Her voice left no doubt this was something she'd been planning for some time. "I'm going to be a missionary. It was always sometime far in the future, something I'd do after—" She bit her lip. "Now Mom's going sooner than I expected. I haven't told her about it, and I'm not going to. It's better she goes away feeling comfortable about my future. She's a terrible worrywart and I can imagine how upset she'd be if I told her I was leaving the security of dear old Canada for South America. To her that's an uncivilized continent of undiscovered tribes in dark jungles."

"Well, it'll certainly be different. But what have you told her about ... about us?" He had to know.

Color rose to Sandy's cheeks and she lowered her head. "I'm afraid I've been somewhat deceitful, but I hope you'll forgive me. In order to reassure her, I've told her we've been talking about marriage and—"

That explained it. "No wonder she told me you're in love with me."

"Please don't hold that against her, Brad," Sandy begged, looking up at him. "I honestly never thought it would reach your ears." She lowered her head again. "I guess it was very naïve of me to think Mom would pass away and this whole thing would remain just between her and me. That it would just disappear into thin air after she died. However, it seems word always gets around. I'm terribly sorry this has caused you worry."

The weight of the last few days lifted off his shoulders. "Sandy, dear, there's nothing you have to apologize for. You've done everything from the goodness of your heart. You had no idea your mother would take things into her own hands to make sure everything was settled before she left." So he only had to play along until Mrs. Davey passed away. "Am I expected to buy you a ring?"

Sandy shook her head. "Oh, no. Nothing like that."

"I kind of got the impression your mother would like there to be a wedding before she..."

Sandy gasped and began to sob. "No, no! Surely not. Oh, Brad, I'm so sorry. It could turn into more of a muddle than I ever imagined."

Brad reached for her and held her against him. It was obvious the charade had escaped from her grasp and got a life of its own, with Mrs. Davey telling the ladies who went to visit her that he and Sandy were as good as engaged. No wonder Mrs. Ericson was so certain of her facts.

Brad held Sandy without a word, comforting her and stroking her hair.

Just then Maggie walked in. She stopped at the threshold and her face went up in flames. "Oh, I'm sorry," she had the presence of mind to say. "I didn't know ... I mean, I didn't mean to disturb you," she stammered.

She began to back out, but Brad signaled for her to stay, while Sandy slipped out of his arms and brushed away the last of her tears.

Damnation! Brad could imagine the gossip this innocent scenario would start among the giggling girls, and then spread out to their families. And to Katharine. She would be the first to hear of this "love scene" and she would be sure to think he was in love with Sandy.

"It's all right, Maggie," Brad said with a calm smile

that belied his dismay. "You didn't interrupt anything." The girl had seen what she'd seen and there was no denying what it had looked like to her. Even if he wanted to, he couldn't reveal the real story behind the hug. What a mess!

"I ... I forgot my running shoes, and I need them for gym tomorrow." Maggie was finally able to speak coherently. "We were on the way home when I noticed I'd left them here. I called Mom and she was pretty annoyed because Beth—that's my babysitter who drove me—had to drive me back for them."

"I'll help you look for them," Sandy offered. "I'm sure they're here somewhere."

"I saw a pair over there," Brad pointed to a corner. "Pink laces?"

Sandy fetched the shoes and handed them to Maggie.

"Yup, they're mine." Maggie took them and turned to go. Brad could tell she was still embarrassed, although there was a little smile on her lips when she called, "Good night," at the door.

Brad figured she was probably making a dash for the car in order to get home quickly to tell her mother what she'd seen. The devil take it all!

After Sandy left, Brad vented his fury on the light switches as he went around snapping them off. It angered him to think Katharine now would be under the impression he and Sandy were lovers.

All at once he stopped, his hand raised to a light switch. Why on earth was he so annoyed? What Katharine thought about him and Sandy made no difference. It didn't matter at all.

Except, somehow it did. Very much.

Chapter Nine

Maggie burst through the door and into the living room, her face flushed with excitement. "Mom, guess what I just saw!" she yelled to Katharine, who was re-clining on the couch resting her leg.

Katharine clamped her hands over her ears. "Mag-gie, for God's sake, calm down."

The girl plunked herself on the floor beside the couch. "You'll never guess."

"Hmm ... now what could have caused this up-heaval?" Katharine mused, smiling at Maggie's excited face. "A spaceship landed on the parking lot?"

Her smile faded when Maggie told her what she'd witnessed.

Hey, everything was cool. All Katharine had to do was take a few deep breaths to get her emotions under control. What Maggie had just seen was not unex-pected. It just proved Brad and Sandy—despite what he'd said about them not being engaged, despite the words he'd said to her, despite the look she'd seen in his eyes—obviously Brad and Sandy were lovers. Maybe they weren't engaged yet, but it looked like they soon would be, just like Mrs. Ericson had foretold.

Time to fetch the old hat back from the ring.

What puzzled Katharine was Brad's emphatic denial of the relationship. Was there some reason why he didn't want it to be generally known? And why was he making a play for Katharine—albeit a small one—behind Sandy's back? That was hardly the sort of behavior she expected from a minister of God. Surely there was something else going on. Curse the man. Why was he being so obscure?

"I hope we can go to church on Sunday," Maggie said, getting up from the floor and heading for her room. "Because I'll miss it if we don't."

"Miss what? I thought you didn't care for the sermons," Katharine said.

"Oh, I'm getting used to them, now that I kinda understand what he's saying a bit more," Maggie called over her shoulder. "And I really like the singing."

Katharine lay back on the couch, her feelings in total confusion. Knowing Brad and Sandy were lovers changed everything about attending the services. If it weren't for Maggie, she would never go again. After all, why bother? Her so-called "plan of attack" no longer mattered. It was a dead issue.

What grieved her most was that the comforting, reassuring feeling Brad's firm handshake would never feel the same again, even if she did continue to attend church. That's what she'd always looked forward to, and that feeling was what she would miss so achingly.

To go or not to go? That was the question.

All Thursday Katharine struggled with whether to attend the choir practice or not. Her knee still gave her more pain than she cared to admit, so it probably would be wise to remain on the couch and watch TV. And staying at home would keep her safely away from Brad, who might show up and force her to witness his show of affection for Sandy. Which would be even more painful than the knee.

But if she continued to go to choir, that was something she'd have to get used to. Defiance rose inside her. She really did enjoy the singing, and no way was she going to allow her messed up feelings for Brad keep her away from an activity she loved. Besides, hadn't she been told Brad never came to choir rehearsals? So more than likely he wouldn't show up there tonight. And since, despite her knee, she was able to drive, she decided she was going, and that was that.

"Make sure you finish your homework before you start to watch TV, Munchkin," she called to Maggie as she picked up her music binder from the deacon's bench in the hall. "Beth will be here soon." She reached for her cane, which she now used, having found the crutches too cumbersome.

"I will. Don't worry, Mom," Maggie hollered from her room. "I just have science to do after my French. Have a nice time singing, and say hi to Pastor Brad and Sandy for me. And be careful with your knee."

"I will. I'll see Sandy, but Pastor Brad won't be there."

She hoped.

At the church, people were slowly assembling on the choir loft, talking and laughing as they found their seats. Katharine's ascent had been slow, but she'd managed surprisingly well with the help of her cane.

Sandy, as always, was chatting with everyone, making each person feel as though he or she was the very reason Sandy had come tonight. Katharine watched her with dismay. Yes, Sandy would make a wonderful wife for a pastor. Too bad it was the same pastor *she* had her eye on. Or *used* to have her eye on.

There were two new songs to learn and Katharine tackled the music with relish. Cantor Jones beamed at her and told her how happy he was she hadn't let the knee keep her away.

As they finished the first song with a rousing final chord, enthusiastic clapping made heads turn toward the door, where Brad stood leaning against the frame.

"Fantastic," he said. "May I stay and listen?"

"Of course, Pastor Brad." Cantor Jones wiped his brow and thumbed through the notes in front of him. He gave directions for the next song, but Katharine failed to hear his words. Her heart thumped too loudly in her ears.

Blast! He came after all. Probably to pick up Sandy after the practice, like last time. Blindly she flipped through the notes, wishing he would leave, so she could concentrate.

She heard Cantor Jones say, "Ready, sing," and as the choir broke into the song, Katharine stared at the words in front of her, which bore little resemblance to the hymn in question. She glanced at Mrs. Hubble's notes beside her, and quietly turned the pages to the correct hymn.

When she finally caught on to the alto part and was able to join in, the song was half over. Cantor Jones gave her a questioning look, but Katharine sent him a reassuring smile. She was okay. In fact, she was just great, thank you very much. And no Brad was going to mess with her singing.

During the break Mrs. Ericson wanted to tell her about a surefire remedy for hay fever. They were joined by two other ladies who brought their teacups over to the table to hear about this wonder cure.

Brad only nodded at this group in passing and said, "Good evening, ladies." Nothing was directed at Katharine, personally. That was just fine. She raised her chin and sipped her coffee. It didn't matter one whit.

Brad joined Sandy and some friends at a table, and Katharine refused to allow herself to look in their direction. They were all laughing and chatting, but it was the sound of his deep laughter that kept her keenly aware of his nearness. Despite everything, she couldn't help wanting to hear it.

After the break Katharine used her knee as an excuse

to leave. It was a legitimate reason, for it was getting quite painful. She should've listened to her body and not come tonight. Served her right for being defiant.

"I think maybe I came out too early," she told Cantor Jones. "I better go home and get this leg up on the couch."

"Do you want someone to drive you home?" Cantor Jones asked with a worried frown.

"Thanks, but I'll be fine," Katharine assured him. "I press the gas pedal and brake with my right foot, you know."

She knew she wasn't fine. Neither physically nor emotionally. She needed to get away from Brad and his disturbing presence. But as she hobbled with her cane toward the exit, a firm hand caught her by the elbow.

"I don't want you driving home with your knee in this shape," Brad said, and without waiting for a reply, he picked her up in his arms and carried her out to the parking lot.

"I'll drive you home in your car," he told her. "John Hopkins will follow in his car and bring me back."

"No, I can't allow that. It's not fair to poor Cantor Jones," Katharine protested. "He needs his tenors."

"They'll survive."

With great care Brad placed Katharine into the passenger seat and got in behind the wheel. As they drove off, the headlights went on in another car in the parking lot and followed them.

Katharine didn't know what to say. Here she'd been trying to avoid him and ended up instead sitting in a car beside him.

"I'm surprised you came tonight," Brad said. "I didn't think your knee would be in any shape for you to go out." His voice wasn't reproachful. Gently he placed a hand on her knee. "Silly girl." He sounded so tender that Katharine had to swallow a sob.

No one had shown her this kind of caring for so long. Brad's words went straight into her heart and broke through the wall of defiance she'd been building there since Maggie had told her about the romantic encounter on Tuesday.

"It felt better at home." Katharine fought to keep her voice from wobbling, but she couldn't keep her eyes from misting.

They drove on in silence for a few blocks, until Brad unexpectedly blurted out, "I imagine Maggie told you she saw Sandy and me hugging on Tuesday night?"

Katharine drew in her breath with surprise. "Y ... yes," she finally stammered. "She did. She said you were ... um ... kissing."

"Sandy was in my arms," Brad said. "So it probably looked like that to Maggie, but we weren't kissing. We were —"

Katharine hastily cut him off. "Please, Brad, you don't have to explain anything. It honestly isn't any of my business."

"I want you to know," Brad insisted. "I was comforting her. We'd just been talking about her mother's impending death and she was very upset and crying."

"Oh."

"You do remember me telling you, when Mrs. Ericson and I were visiting you, that Sandy and I are *not* engaged?"

"Yes," Katharine whispered.

"That's still true, no matter what Maggie may have told you. We're not going to get married."

"You're not?" Her voice wasn't picking up any volume, but her heart was certainly picking up speed.

"No, we're not," Brad said firmly. "There's something I want to explain to you that may sound a bit incredible. This is not known around the church, so please don't mention it anywhere." He turned to look at her and she nodded. "You see, Sandy's mother desperately wants us to get married and Sandy doesn't have the heart to tell her the truth. I guess you could say Mrs. Davey is very overprotective of her only daughter, and feels that Sandy needs a husband to take care of her. She's convinced I'm the one. Sandy doesn't want to upset her in her last days by arguing with her and telling her the truth. She wants her mother to die in peace."

"Oh." It did sound incredible. Incredibly wonderful. Katharine's heartbeat turned into a happy tattoo.

"I know some people would say it's wrong to let her die believing something that's not going to happen," Brad mused. "But I think it's the right thing to do."

"I guess at this point it's no use upsetting her." Katharine was glad she was finally able to say something reasonably sensible. Her heart continued to celebrate and pumped happiness into every fiber of her body. It made her feel incredibly alive.

"No, there isn't. So I would really appreciate it if you didn't say anything to anyone about this. I know Maggie will be telling everyone about how we were kissing and hugging, and naturally she'll think we're going to get married. For the time being that's okay. However —" Brad stopped speaking and turned his head toward her. Under a streetlight she could see his earnest dark eyes looking deep into hers. "I wanted you to know the truth."

Why? Did he care for her, after all? Was she foolish to hope he was interested in her? He'd been so off and on with her that she was as confused as her old hat. If it wasn't Sandy holding him back, then what?

However, the door was open once again to all the possibilities she'd dreamed of, and she was going to give it one more shot. In the darkness she smiled. Only a few moments ago things had been so hopeless, and now the sun was shining in the middle of the night.

Back in the ring, went the tattered old hat!

Katharine hadn't been able to go to school all week. With the help of her cane she managed to hobble around the apartment and do a few chores, but mostly her days were spent working on the neglected sand and water activities for June, the last month of the school year.

On Sunday afternoon, to her great delight, Brad called to enquire if it would be all right for him to drop over and look in on her.

"It's part of the church's home-visitation program," he explained. Okay, so that wasn't exactly what Katharine wanted to hear, but if that brought him over, she wasn't complaining.

Brad appeared that evening carrying a bouquet of spring flowers and some beef stroganoff Mrs. Ericson had sent with him. He handed Maggie the casserole, and gave the flowers to Katharine who, as usual, was half-reclining on the couch, her leg propped up by a pillow.

She unwrapped the cheerful bouquet. "Tulips and daffodils," she exclaimed. "And irises. How beautiful. Thank you, Brad."

"You're welcome, Katharine." Her name sounded beautiful coming from his lips and made her hope they could soon take the relationship another step closer.

"I saw the flowers in a shop near the church and I immediately thought of you," Brad told her.

"Why did you think of Mom, Pastor Brad?" Maggie asked the very question that was on Katharine's lips.

"Your mother's a very pretty woman, don't you think, Maggie?" Brad said lightly, and Katharine was glad she had the bouquet to fuss over, so her flaming cheeks were hidden. "She's even prettier than these flowers."

"Yep. I think so, too." Maggie agreed. She took the flowers from her mother and carried them into the kitchen to put into a vase.

"Mrs. Ericson was worried you two might not be getting proper food, so she sent the stew," Brad said. "It's delicious. I can vouch for it because I was there for dinner tonight."

Outside the late spring evening was drawing to a close. Earlier, Maggie had lit some candles and put on soft music, and on a side table a single lamp cast a warm glow into the room.

Maggie reappeared with the flowers in a crystal vase, which she placed on the side table near Katharine. Tea was brewing in a little white ceramic pot, and cups and saucers were set out on the coffee table in front of the couch. Maggie had, once again, bought doughnuts, with Katharine's permission.

"Pastor Brad loves them," Maggie had insisted. "And I do, too."

She now grabbed a doughnut from the platter and struck her brow dramatically with the back of her hand. "I shall now betake me to my nocturnal chamber and attack my English homework," she announced. "Shakespeah." She then floated like a tragic heroine out of the room, closing the door behind her.

Laughing, Brad settled into an armchair across from Katharine. "Quite the dramatist."

"Yes, she certainly is."

"How's the knee coming along?"

"Better each day, but not the greatest yet. I hope I'll be able to hobble to school next week," Katharine said. "Luckily I don't need the left leg when I drive. There's something to be said for automatic transmission." She reached for a cup and held it out for him. "Would you mind?"

While he poured the tea, she gazed at him longingly and couldn't help imagining how his sensitive, long fingers would feel caressing her. With his head bent over the task, the lock of hair fell onto his forehead just the way she'd always imagined it would, ever since she'd seen his photo. Even his forbidding clerical collar failed to bring her errant thoughts under control.

He handed her the hors d'oeuvres and then reached for the inevitable doughnut. "Maggie's been shopping,

I see." He smiled as he bit into one.

Katharine returned his smile. "She didn't want you to feel deprived."

A small careless movement of her leg caused her to grimace in pain.

His eyes, dark blue in the dim light, flashed with concern. "Have you been in much discomfort?"

"Some. This knee will take its own sweet time to heal and there's no use rushing it."

"Cantor Jones was so pleased you came to the choir practice, but now he's worried you overexerted yourself. He was praising you to the skies again just the other day."

Katharine couldn't help grinning with pleasure. "He's totally exaggerating and probably secretly wishes my knee would keep me away."

"Well, if that turns out to be the case, I can always arrange to have it retwisted."

Katharine was delighted Brad felt comfortable enough to indulge in a bit of teasing. It made things less formal.

She laughed. "Oh, that's horrible coming from a man of cloth."

The deep, rich sound of his laughter filled the dim room. How she loved to hear it. How she wanted to hear it forever.

Brad leaned forward and rested his elbows on his knees. "So," he then said out of the blue. "Tell me about yourself. What were you like as a little girl?"

Taken aback by this new turn in the conversation, Katharine gave a short, surprised laugh. "Why would you want to know that?"

Because you are always on my mind, Brad wanted to say. Because she filled his days so completely it was difficult to concentrate on anything else.

Instead he said, "Well, since we're friends..." Day and night he thought about her. No matter how he tried to distract himself. White bear. White bear.

Katharine. Katharine.

"Are we friends?" There was a smile in her question.

"Yes. I mean ... I *hope* we are." Boy, that was so lame.

"Of course." She aimed her incredible eyes at him. Bedroom eyes.

Brad wanted to reach out and touch her hand as it rested on the couch beside her. "You're very beautiful," he said before he could stop himself. "I mean, tonight," he quickly amended. "You're beautiful tonight," he tried again, but that didn't sound any better. He felt like an idiot.

Katharine's surprised laughter bubbled out. "Beautiful tonight? But not usually?"

Brad squirmed inwardly. Why was he behaving like such a dork? "Beautiful, always," he muttered.

She gave him a teasing smile. "Do you say that to all the women in the church?"

He shook his head. "Of course not." That's the kind of insufferable stuff he *used* to say to all the women in his life. Only now, when he said it to her, he meant it. It wasn't just a line to get her into bed.

"I'll bet you do. That's why they say such nice things about you."

"What nice things do they say?"

"I'm sure you've heard."

"I haven't, but you could fill me in, and make me feel insufferably vain." Smiling, he crossed his arms, ready to listen.

"Well, I overheard two women named Ethel and Jean talking about your sermons. Apparently you make these ladies feel *so* good. They especially like the ones where you say our sins are forgiven if we show sincere remorse."

That's exactly where he didn't want to go. His hypocrisy almost made him nauseous. "The ladies tend to exaggerate, my dear. You mustn't take everything you hear as gospel truth."

"Well, I guess then I'll have to take your sermons with a grain of salt, too," she joked, oblivious to how her words affected him.

"Yes," he said. "*Especially* my sermons." He clenched his jaws. The hypocritical sermons that he, himself, didn't believe. Katharine looked at him with a puzzled frown. Of course she wouldn't know how to interpret his words. To distract her, he poured himself more tea. "Would you like some, too?"

"Please." Katharine still looked somewhat taken aback.

For a moment they sat in silence, and he could see she was trying to figure out what had just happened.

"So what exactly did you want to know about me?" she finally asked.

Brad was happy she brought the conversation back to its original track. He relaxed and leaned back in his chair. "How about everything?"

Katharine lifted one finger. "I was an only child and a spoiled brat."

"I don't believe that," he countered. "Spoiled brats grow into selfish adults and you're such a nice person that it can't be true. Next."

"I was a plain, overweight teenager," she said, holding up another finger.

"Can't be true. You're so beautiful now, you must have been a gorgeous teenager."

Yes, he would have had to be dead not to take in the curvaceous lines of her figure as she lay, half-reclined, on the couch. Was this woman completely oblivious to the wild storms she roused in him? Surely she had to see the admiration in his eyes, because there was no way he could hide it, unless he stared at the walls.

The soft, dreamlike music and candlelight were a magical combination and he forced his eyes to return to her face. That was no better. Now the aquamarine green of her eyes threatened to drown him. He tried to grasp onto some fragment of sanity but failed. The feelings he'd suppressed for weeks now forced their way to the surface like scorching lava from a volcano. He wanted nothing in the world but to lie down on the couch and crush this woman against him, and lose himself inside her beauty.

"Katharine." His voice was thick with emotion. And then, because he needed to touch her, Brad reached out and took her hand and brought it to his lips, kissing her palm.

Her surprised gasp brought him back to sanity. Though he wanted to bend over and do the same to her lips, instead he reluctantly freed her hand and leaned back in his chair. His guts were in turmoil for the axis of his world had just completed a major upheaval.

He glanced at his watch and stretched his legs. "Gosh, I didn't realize how late it was." He stood up. "I'd better be on my way. You and your knee need to rest."

Brad walked to the front door and his hand trembled as he helped himself to his jacket from the hook. He gripped the doorknob, but then turned around and returned.

"Maggie, I'm leaving," he called to the closed door of her room. "Good night!"

Maggie poked her head out. "Good night, Pastor Brad. See you soon." She withdrew back into her room.

Brad was about to go out, but again he turned and came back to stand beside the couch.

"Good-bye, Katharine," he said and held out his hand. It was steady now, but his heart was sad with regret. He was forced leave and put an end to something he instead, so desperately, wanted to begin.

She hesitated before offering her hand to him. The confused look in her eyes confirmed the signals he was sending to her were anything but clear. He could have kicked himself for what he had just done. If she only knew how much he wanted to hold her, to kiss her —

Katharine's smile was strained, but her voice was light and whimsical when she said, "Don't you mean good night, Brad? Good-bye sounds so final, like I won't ever see you again."

He tried his best to return her smile. "Of course I meant good night."

No, he didn't. He meant good-bye. Good-bye to the love he could never have. He kept holding her hand.

"I'll tell you all about my childhood next time," she said. "And maybe you can tell me about your past."

He flinched. "Right." Sure he would. All about his horrible deeds.

"I'll drop by to see you again." He swallowed. He didn't want to, but he released her hand and then quickly turned and closed the door firmly behind him.

The devil take it all!

Chapter Ten

Maggie beamed and importantly nodded left and right, as she and Katharine made their way slowly down the aisle on Sunday.

"We're like a couple of celebrities," Maggie whispered, acknowledging the sympathetic looks directed at Katharine, who limped along with her cane.

"No, we're not," Katharine said out of the corner of her mouth. "So stop behaving like some member of royalty." She only hoped Maggie wouldn't start waving.

"I'm just responding to their kindness, Mom," Maggie explained. "I thought you'd be pleased I'm being polite."

Katharine laughed. "Polite I can understand, but this is just a bit over the top."

They hadn't been to church since the accident. On her doctor's orders Katharine had spent the days following the choir practice letting her knee have a good rest.

Although she would have liked to sing with the choir today, she had decided to forego the climb up to the loft.

Brad hadn't dropped by to see her again, as he'd promised. Nor had he called. She couldn't help feeling disappointed, although "confused" would have better described her feelings.

When he visited a week ago, and kissed her hand, she'd been certain he was about to take her in his arms and kiss her lips. There was such a look of desire his eyes that her head still spun when she thought of it. And when he'd whispered her name, the atmosphere had been so charged it could have lit all the light bulbs in the room. She'd totally expected the words "I love you" to follow.

Nothing. Just, "Good-bye".

Yet, he had to know how he affected her. Surely mature adults could read between the lines when a relationship was ready to go up another notch.

But did they even have a relationship? She'd thought they did, but now, after his visit with his puzzling, abrupt withdrawal from a promising, romantic overture, she was no longer sure.

Irritation boiled inside her. What right had he to jerk her around like this? Why didn't he acknowledge his attraction for her and behave like a lover? Or then stop looking at her like she was something special to him. This just wasn't fair.

"Do you think Pastor Brad'll come and sit with us downstairs?" Maggie asked as they reached the fifth row and slipped into their customary pew. "He didn't come to visit you again."

"I told you, Pastor Brad is a busy man," Katharine said. "We do *not* own him, although you seem to think we do. Besides, when he visited me he saw my knee was coming along just fine. There was no need for him to get a daily update, for goodness sake. It's just a knee. There are people in the congregation who are really sick, and even dying. He has to visit them."

"Yeah, sure." Maggie's mouth, pulled down in a grimace, indicated that in her opinion Pastor Brad had neglected his duties.

Brad entered shortly and knelt at the altar, his head bowed in prayer. His white embroidered alb flowed smoothly down his broad back. After a minute he rose, turned to face the congregation, and raised his hand in blessing.

"I know some of the answers we have to give," Maggie whispered proudly as she leafed through the book for the opening hymn. "And I can sing some of the songs."

"Hymns," Katharine corrected her.

"Same diff. But I wish there weren't so many of them. I'll never be able to learn them all."

"Shh." Her mother nudged her lightly with her arm. "You're forgetting the church is like a library. You have to be quiet."

The organ gave the introduction and the congregation joined in. It was one of the old, familiar hymns Katharine had loved to sing in her childhood and now she let her voice ring out freely. She could see Brad singing, but the organ and Cantor Jones boomed above all, drowning out the competition.

She observed Brad as he did "the singing and the talking", as Maggie called it. Although he scanned the congregation from time to time during the sermon, not once did he look their way.

Katharine squared her shoulders. All right. If what happened during his visit didn't mean a thing to him, she was just fine with that.

No, she wasn't.

She gazed at him at the altar and couldn't prevent her heart from filling with longing. Why couldn't things be simple? Either he was attracted to her or he wasn't. She just wanted to know.

At the end of the service Brad made a couple of announcements about forthcoming church activities. A car wash fundraiser was scheduled for the following Saturday at the church parking lot.

"We're going, aren't we, Mom?" Maggie whispered with excitement. "I've never done a car wash before."

"I'll think about it," Katharine whispered.

The Women's Prayer Group would be holding a bake

sale, and again Katharine felt Maggie's elbow nudging her.

"That's a good one for you, Mom," the girl whispered.

"And why so?"

"You bake a mean apple pie. They'll sell like anything."

"Thank you, but I'm not in the Prayer Group," Katharine pointed out.

"They said any contributions are welcome, didn't you hear?"

"I'll think about it."

They filed down the aisle after the worship, Katharine hobbling with her cane.

"Did you want to go and have a glass of juice downstairs?" Katharine asked. She knew Maggie always enjoyed that.

Maggie puckered her lips. "I don't know," she mused. "Since Pastor Brad doesn't care about your knee, he probably won't even come and sit with us."

Katharine burst out laughing. "You're hopeless! Of course he won't come and sit with us. I told you, you can't think of him as our personal property. He belongs to all these people here."

As usual, Brad was at the door, but instead of giving him her bubbling greeting, Maggie merely said a cool, "Hello."

Brad looked a bit taken aback by this but, as usual, he greeted her warmly.

His, "Hello, Mrs. Wilder, nice to see you," on the other hand, sounded only lukewarm.

After the recent events, this didn't surprise Katharine. Nothing about him surprised her any more. Puzzled her, yes. Surprised her, no. One moment he seemed ready to plunge into a relationship—into love, even—and the next he was pushing her away, as though she was Typhoid Mary.

They went downstairs, although halfway there the

knee told her it probably wasn't the smartest idea. However, she soldiered on and sat down at their usual table. Without even being asked, Maggie brought her a cup of coffee and got herself some juice. Taking care of her mother was helping Maggie mature, Katharine had observed.

After what had happened lately, she was totally unprepared to see Brad come walking toward their table, carrying his coffee cup.

"May I join you?" he asked and, without waiting for an answer, pulled out a chair and seated himself.

Katharine's pulse went into overdrive and hammered at her temples. *Cut it out, you silly heart,* she told herself, but that failed to stop the pounding.

"How's your knee doing?" Brad asked. "I've been thinking about you."

Sure he had. His false words finally helped to normalize her heartbeat. "It's much better, thank you," she replied.

"That's great. You'll be able to return to school soon?"

"Yes, tomorrow." Katharine was determined not to make things easy for him by engaging in friendly chatter. He didn't deserve it.

"That's good. Maggie can be freed from her nursemaid duties."

Maggie sat, a picture of aloofness, sipping her juice and munching on a cookie, making it obvious Brad was in her bad books.

"So, Maggie, what have you been up to all week?" Brad asked, patting her hand in a conciliatory gesture.

"I've been mostly helping Mom and doing schoolwork," Maggie replied in cool tones. "And what have *you* been up to all week, Pastor Brad?"

Brad's brows shot up in surprise. "I've been busy with church work," he replied.

To Katharine his voice sounded defensive, and she wondered if Maggie was astute enough to discern it, too.

"Like visiting the sick and dying and stuff like that?" It was easy to see where Maggie was going with this.

"Yes, things like that."

"We have a sick person in *our* home, too." Maggie pointed out the obvious.

"I know. And I tried to find the time to come and see her again."

Katharine winced. Like hell he did! He didn't come because of what happened at his last visit. Frankly, it was good he hadn't shown up, because his mixed signals were driving her crazy and she might have flung the tea at him instead of offering it to him.

"Yeah. Mom told me you're *very* busy."

Katharine heard the censure in Maggie's reply. Obviously Brad did, too, for his eyes flashed and the look he shot at Katharine said "guilty as charged".

"I guess I should at least have phoned," he said to Maggie. "I'm very sorry I've been neglectful."

As soon as she heard his apology, Maggie gave him a forgiving smile.

"That's okay. I'm going to get another cookie. Do you want one, Mom? Pastor Brad?"

They both shook their heads.

As soon as Maggie was out of earshot, Brad turned to Katharine. His voice was barely audible. "I didn't come because —"

"Yes?" She could have let him off the hook by saying polite things like she understood, or it was all right, but after the way he'd been tossing her about, she didn't feel very generous.

"I'm sorry. I was totally out of line."

"Were you? I didn't notice." Yes, she was being a bitch.

He looked surprised at her caustic tone. "I don't know why I—" To cover his embarrassment he lowered his head and gulped down some coffee.

"Why you what?" Katharine asked, her voice hard

as nails.

When he looked up, he said in a firm voice, "It won't happen again. I promise."

"What won't?" Katharine pressed on unwaveringly. She was in no mood for his games.

At that point Maggie returned to the table, shutting off any further talk and Brad rose, leaving Katharine sitting, her jaws clenched in anger.

He turned to smile at the people at the next table. "Duty calls," he said to them, and turned back to Maggie. "I'll see you on Tuesday night, right?"

"Uh-huh." Maggie nodded and wiped cookie crumbs off her face with the back of her hand.

Brad then turned to face Katharine. "Thank you for your company, Mrs. Wilder," he said politely. "I hope the knee will soon be as good as new. Good-bye."

He was gone, and again he'd said "Good-bye".

Although the word created a hard knot where her heart used to be, Katharine forced herself to ignore the pain. She wanted to leave, but was forced to sit there while Maggie chatted on about the car wash.

Katharine stared blankly at her empty coffee cup. Things were getting more and more confusing, despite her attempt to get them straightened out. There was something he didn't want to tell her. Was he impotent? Was he just not into women? Was there something in his past he couldn't share? She wanted him just to *tell* her, for God's sake, so at last she could understand.

Finally Katharine used her knee as an excuse to leave.

"It's starting to hurt," she said. It wasn't. But her heart was, despite her attempts to ignore it.

Katharine returned to school on Monday to the unbridled joy of her grade ones. She knew they didn't transfer their loyalties very easily to a substitute teacher, no matter how kind and capable the person was. As she stood at the classroom door greeting her pupils, she was deluged with hugs and happy cries.

"Mrs. Wilder's back!"

"I missed you, Mrs. Wilder."

A shy little girl, whom she'd had much difficulty in reaching this year, came up to Katharine and put her arms around her waist. "I'm glad you're back," the child whispered. In her smudged fist she held a crumpled bunch of dandelion blooms, which she thrust at Katharine.

Katharine smiled and tousled the girl's dark, windblown hair. "These are lovely flowers. Thank you, dear."

She put the blossoms into a shallow glass dish she kept for just such offerings.

"There can't be another occupation in this world where you get such sincere, unconditional loving," Katharine confided to Bonnie during recess. They sat in the staff lounge drinking a quick cup of coffee.

"That's why I only teach the primary grades," Bonnie confessed. "They fill a need in my lonely life."

"Lonely? Broo-haa!" Katharine brayed. "You're always on the go with one beau or another."

"But I have no children of my own," Bonnie said, almost managing to look depressed. "Did I tell you about the time I got on a bus and saw a man I thought I recognized. 'Aren't you the father of one of my children?' I asked him, and for a while I couldn't figure out why people were staring at us, and why the man blushed and quickly slunk off to the rear of the bus."

Katharine laughed. "Poor guy."

The bell rang and she poured her unfinished coffee into the sink. As they headed back to their classrooms, Bonnie slowed down to keep pace with Katharine, who still walked with the cane, not trusting the knee completely.

"So are you going to your church choir again this week?" Bonnie asked. She had grumbled several times

about Katharine's "religious conversion", as she mock-
ingly called it. "You're getting so caught up in those
church activities one never sees you anymore. We're
having a clothing party at my place on Thursday night
and there'll be some really fantastic outfits you should
try on."

"Try on is about all I'd be able to do. I can't afford
another outfit right now. Besides, Maggie would go totally ballistic if I bought any more clothes."

"You're letting that daughter of yours have way too
much say in your financial affairs," Bonnie admonished her. "Let's face it, you're just afraid if you're too
hard on her, she's going to want to go live with Ted."

"Stop nagging me, Bonnie," Katharine countered
jokingly. "You're as bad as Maggie. Besides, she's quite
right in this case. You know what we teachers earn."

They had reached Katharine's classroom door. "And
yes, I'll continue going to the choir. I really love singing
there."

Katharine sighed as she entered her class. Bonnie
was right. She probably *was* too easy on Maggie in
order to keep her from leaving. Of course at this point
Maggie was too young to make that decision, but what
if one day ... ?

An enthusiastic group of young people and several
adults were already at the church parking lot on Saturday morning, when Maggie and Katharine drove up.
To Maggie's delight, the car wash day had dawned
sunny and bright after two rainy days.

"We'll have a gazillion cars to wash," she enthused,
pulling out a supply of rags from a bag. "All that mud
everywhere."

Katharine took a bucket and a vacuum cleaner out
of the trunk and handed them to Maggie. She then
pulled out two large sheets of cardboard and markers,
and started to make herself a sandwich board. At this

point, parading slowly back and forth at the nearest intersection, waving prospective customers to the car wash, was the best job for her. Her knee was no longer giving her too much trouble, but washing cars might still strain it.

"I'll volunteer my car as a guinea pig. You can practice your washing technique on it. For free, of course," she offered.

"Forget it, Mom," Maggie countered as she slipped on a huge, oversized Tee shirt and got her gear ready for action. "No freebies here. You want your car washed, you pay for it."

"That's hardly fair," Katharine grumbled. "Here I am, giving up my Saturday and subjecting myself to the humiliation of being a walking advertisement, and I don't even get a free car wash out of it. I hereby voice my objection."

She finished writing up the sign and attached some string to go over her shoulders. The billboard flapped around, hitting her on the behind and bouncing off her breast as she walked toward the intersection.

The late June morning was already heating up, promising a sweltering hot and humid day. Katharine had tied her long, auburn hair up in a ponytail, and wore a bright yellow tee shirt and khaki walking shorts. She began to stroll slowly up and down the sidewalk, and gradually warmed up to the job, so that before long she was even waving her arms with a show of enthusiasm.

She wondered whether Brad was going to show up today, although it made no difference whatsoever to her whether he did or not—or so she told her hopeful heart. There had been no contact since Sunday, for Brad hadn't shown up at the Thursday's choir rehearsal. Thank goodness for that. Katharine had been able to enjoy the singing without his disturbing presence.

She was the only person working the intersection,

but had been promised a companion as soon as more people showed up. After a half hour of pacing, she began to feel the need for something to drink, and tried to get the attention of the kids who were busily washing two cars on the parking lot. They ignored her waving, probably thinking she was just trying to attract customers and were too far away for her to call.

She had already resigned herself to not having any refreshments, when Brad came sauntering toward her holding two paper cups. Although she couldn't stop her heart from a doing wild flip, she strove to steel herself and keep her voice casual.

"Hello, Pastor," she said. "That's for me, I hope."

"Yes, I was sent to give it to you." He handed her the cup. "Some iced tea."

"Thanks. No sugar?"

"Sorry. There's sugar in it."

"That's all right. To tell you the truth, I really prefer my tea sweet and only avoid sugar because of the extra calories." This was safe, idle talk that allowed her to remain distant without being unfriendly. They were adults, after all, and had to get along despite the abrupt, disconcerting way their last meeting had ended.

"I don't think you need to worry about calories," he commented, taking a gulp of tea. Then, grinning mischievously he said, "You know, that outfit of yours sure is pretty suggestive."

Katharine's eyes flew open in surprise.

Brad pointed to her sign. "I meant the sandwich board, of course. It's suggesting people should come for a car wash."

Katharine laughed. His joking helped to wash away the tension and anger she had harbored inside her since his awkward apology was left hanging in the air between them—apology for having shown her he cared, for God's sake! As if that was something he needed to apologize for.

When he'd said good-bye, it made her think they would never again be on friendly terms, and yet, here he was, joking and laughing as if that unfortunate situation had never happened. Her resolve dissolved like so many snowflakes falling on a pond and she couldn't prevent the friendly, warm feelings from rising in her breast towards him. It was just so much nicer having an easy conversation with him than standing there tight-lipped and scowling.

And then he proposed something that made the day turn even sunnier.

"I was thinking," Brad mused, "that one of these days we should have a meeting and talk about your role at the summer camp."

Katharine hesitated for only a second. She didn't want to turn down this chance to be with him. Despite his annoying, erratic behavior, hope stuck its head out from wherever it lurked inside her, whispering that maybe this time she would finally get an answer. Maybe she would discover how to solve this conundrum known as Brad Scott. Maybe there was a possibility, after all, to have a relationship with him.

Or was she just a silly cock-eyed optimist?

"I think that would be useful. I haven't been to a camp since I was a kid, and in those days my responsibilities consisted of having fun and staying out of trouble."

"That's what I thought. When do you think you could swing it?"

"Probably next week," she suggested. "How's Monday night?"

"Do you like seafood?" Brad asked. "There's a restaurant I like downtown by the lake. It's called Captain Mel's."

Katharine burst into laughter. "I'm going to get a dinner out of this? That a nice bonus."

"I just thought a downtown restaurant will be more private for having a conversation," Brad explained."

Better than some local coffee shop where we might run
into church members who would be surprised to see
us together, chatting tête-à-tête. You know, with Mrs.
Davey —"

"Yes, of course," she agreed.

Just then Sandy came up the sidewalk, also sport-
ing a sandwich board. "Hi, Katharine!" she called.
"You're really bringing in the business." She turned to
Brad. "I'm afraid you have to stop flirting with the help
and get back to the base. They need you to oversee the
vacuuming. I think the kids are doing a Seven Dwarfs
routine and hiding the dirt under the floor mats."

"Can't have that." Brad turned to go. "I'll talk to you
later, Katharine."

After Brad had gone, Katharine and Sandy proceeded to walk side by side up and down the sidewalk.

"Brad just suggested he and I should meet and talk
about the summer camp," Katharine began. She and
Sandy hadn't had a chance to speak since Brad had
made the revelation about Sandy's mother.

"Probably a good idea," Sandy said in her usual
bright and cheerful way. "There are a lot of details
about the camp you aren't familiar with."

"He suggested we go to a restaurant," Katharine
continued, testing the waters. How would Sandy react
to this meeting that almost sounded like a date?

"Hey, you might as well get a good meal out of this
volunteering business," Sandy said, with a laugh.
"There's not much else you'll be getting."

Katharine decided to put all her cards on the table.
"We'll be going to a restaurant downtown so there
won't be any possible gossiping about us, since—you
understand."

Sandy nodded. "Of course. Because of my mother,
right?"

"Yes. The word might get around that Brad was
seen with me, instead of you, and set the tongues wagging."

Sandy placed a hand on Katharine's arm. "I'm so sorry you're going to such trouble because of me. I'm afraid I didn't foresee all the possible consequences of my actions."

"That's all right," Katharine said. "You were only being kind."

"I just never thought Brad would become so fond of someone." Sandy looked Katharine in the eye. "I've known Brad for several years, and in all that time he's never shown any signs of falling in love. Not till now. And I should know because he's been like a brother to me. And that's why I'm so sorry I'm throwing a wrench into his plans. Because of me he can't just openly court you."

As Sandy spoke, Katharine's heart picked up speed until it was almost racing out of her chest. Brad was falling in love with her? So it wasn't just her imagination.

She put out a feeler. "I don't think Brad has any so-called 'plans' with regards to me," she protested. "He's never said anything."

Sandy begged to differ. "He certainly does, whether he's said anything to you or not. I know the man. I've observed him when you're around and there's no denying he has feelings for you."

"You think?" Katharine's voice held a quaver of hope she couldn't hide.

"I *know*," Sandy said firmly. "And being the kind of guy he is, having had no romantic involvement with women all these years—or maybe never—he's probably a bit slow on the uptake. You just have to encourage him, that's all."

"I can't imagine such a good-looking man never having had a romantic involvement," Katharine countered. "He's not a priest, after all." Thank goodness.

"Well, I may be wrong on that account," Sandy confessed. "But all the time I've known him, he's never even looked at a woman with stars in his eyes. Not until now."

"So why're you getting all dolled up tonight, Mom?" Maggie asked. She sat cross-legged on Katharine's bed observing her mother's moves with interest. It obviously hadn't escaped her notice that Katharine was taking more care with her dress and make-up than she normally did for a night out with friends.

Katharine tried to keep her reply light and playful. "It's summer. I want to look fresh and pretty for a change."

"So what's the occasion?"

It was a perfectly innocent question. No reason for Katharine to get irritated by it. They always were up on each other's comings and goings, but tonight Katharine obviously couldn't let Maggie know she was having dinner with Brad, even if she were to present it strictly as a business meeting. Which it obviously was, because Brad hadn't called it a date when they'd finalized the plans a few days ago. Still, Katharine could hope, couldn't she? Especially after what Sandy had told her.

The guilt over the need to lie to Maggie made her defensive. "I'm just getting together with some teachers. Nothing special."

"Well, I bet some male teacher is joining you," Maggie teased, with a sly grin. "The way you are fussing with your make-up and all."

"Please stop this silly talk!" Katharine snapped. "I told you I just want to get dressed up for a change. Anything wrong with that?"

Without a word, Maggie slid off the bed and slunk out of the room.

Dear Lord! Maggie had only been playful. Why did she have to react so angrily? Filled with remorse, Katharine followed Maggie into the living room where the girl was sulking in the armchair. Her arms were crossed on her chest and her chin was sunk defiantly low on her chest.

"I'm really, really sorry, sweetie," Katharine whispered to the hunched back. She took a hold of Maggie's shoulders. "I don't know why I snapped at you like that. I didn't mean to."

The girl turned around slowly and grimaced at Katharine. "Maybe you have a guilty conscience, Mom?"

Katharine blanched, but Maggie continued, unaware she'd hit a raw nerve. "I think there really *is* a man at this get-together and you're interested in him, but you don't want to tell me. That's what *I* think."

She was almost on target. What an uncanny way the child had of reading Katharine's thoughts.

"Don't worry, Mom," Maggie went on. "It's okay for you to have dates. After all, Daddy's been married for years, now. It's about time you found someone, too."

Although Katharine was very cognizant of Shakespeare's warning about tangled webs, she carried on with her lie. She smiled. "You've hit the nail on the head, Munchkin, and seen through my little game."

"So, who's the guy?" Maggie asked. Her eyes now sparkled with excitement. "Anyone I know?"

"You've never seen him at any of the school functions." Well, at least *that* was the truth. "He's retired." That was not.

"Retired," Maggie scoffed in dismay. "You're too young and pretty to go with a retired man, Mom."

"I'm not *going* with anyone, darling. I'm simply having dinner." She turned to go as the buzzer sounded. "That's Beth. Tell her there's spaghetti for the two of you in the fridge."

"Okay, Mom. And you *should* go out more often, you know. You look fabulous, all made up and dressed fancy."

"Thanks, sweetie. I'm glad you approve."

Katharine took the subway train downtown, as she

usually did, for parking wasn't easy to find in the city core and was too costly for her budget anyway. All the way down the wheels of the train clicked, "Brad is waiting, Brad is waiting". Impatiently she counted the stops, and at last the train pulled up at the final station by the lake. She got off, ran up the escalator, and out onto the street.

The soft evening breeze blew in from the lake as she hurried toward the restaurant. The streetlights, fashioned after old gas lamps, were already lit cast their sparkling reflections in the water.

Suddenly she was fully conscious of what was about to happen. She was meeting Brad for dinner. This was a date with a man who was falling in love with her—at least according to Sandy. The closer she got to the lake—and Brad—the harder Katharine prayed Sandy was right.

"Captain Mel's" was an old lake schooner, which now was anchored solidly beside the pier, transformed into a fine seafood restaurant. As she approached it, she saw Brad leaning leisurely against the wall by the open door, waiting. When he saw her, he raised an arm in greeting and came down the gangplank to meet her.

Instead of his clerical collar, tonight he wore a sports jacket, tie, and dark pants. He held out his hand to her, and her fingers slipped naturally into it, just as they had the first time they'd met in church. Again she had the same feeling of comfort and warmth, as though she'd arrived home.

"I was afraid you might've changed your mind," he said. "Being a school night, I thought maybe you decided it wasn't a good idea. I wanted to call, but —"

"I'm sorry I'm late," Katharine gasped. She was out of breath, but didn't know if it was from hurrying, or from being so close to him. "I had to wait for the train longer than I expected."

"That seems to be the case more and more often these days. Well, shall we go in?" He didn't release her hand as he guided her into the restaurant and informed the hostess of their reservation. Katharine was intensely aware of his touch and found it difficult to normalize her breathing. Did he feel, like she, that it was just plain wonderful to touch? As they walked to their table, he put his hand on her back in a gesture of courtesy, and his fingers burned into her, down to her very bones. It was a delicious scorching that only made her want more.

Their table was in a secluded corner, by a large window overlooking the lake. He held out the chair for her and then sat down opposite her.

When the waiter came, Brad ordered the wine, and they began to peruse their menus. He'd been here before and was able to make some suggestions. After ordering, they sat back and surveyed the darkening lake before them. Katharine relished the sense of intimacy this little nook offered. Had he reserved it for this reason? Was he also feeling this same sense of closeness?

Brad smiled. In the candlelight his dark eyes were almost black, and the fires gleaming in their depths sent shivers of excitement through her.

"You look lovely," he said. "And you brought a beautiful evening with you."

Self-consciously Katharine brushed a hand over her hair. "I think you have better connections to the Man Above than I. But thank you. You're looking very elegant, yourself."

The waiter brought the wine and, after Brad had approved it, poured some for each of them.

Katharine held up her glass in a salute. "To a lovely evening and a productive meeting," she said, although discussing the camp was the last thing she wanted to do tonight.

Chapter Eleven

Brad wanted to reach over and touch her hand, but any gestures that might be construed as even remotely romantic could throw a kibosh on the real reason he'd asked her to come. It wasn't to talk about the camp, although she thought it was. It was to apologize for having given her the false idea that this relationship could evolve into something romantic. That it had a future.

On the lake the sailboats skimmed dream-like over the quiet water. The evening breeze was light, barely filling the sails, but no one seemed to be in a hurry to go anywhere. The red and green masthead lights reflected on the water, adding their sparkle to the myriad white lights that twinkled in the harbor. If only he and Katharine could sail away in one of those boats to some distant land, far from everything that kept him from loving her, but he knew he could never get away from his past and the promise he'd made. That would follow him to the ends of the earth. So it was best to nip this relationship in the bud. Of course this was too late for him because he would always love her and miss her. But at least she would be spared the pain of a broken love affair for she—he hoped—wasn't really in love with him.

They sat playing with their wine until Brad broke

the silence. "A penny for your thoughts," he said with a smile.

Katharine returned his smile. "I didn't know people still said things like that."

"I just did."

"My thoughts —" Katharine hesitated. "On a lovely night like this, my thoughts are on —"

"Yes?" Brad reached for her hand across the table. He couldn't help it, even if it went against everything he'd just been telling himself.

Katharine didn't pull away. "I was thinking —" she began again, but stopped.

"Yes?" he prompted again.

Katharine took a deep breath and swallowed, as though forcing down a constricting lump.

"Since Sandy isn't a deterrent for us to be together," she blurted out. "And I love y —"

"Don't!" he rasped, as dark panic filled him. She must never say those words.

Katharine snatched her hand away, her face reflecting the dismay she was feeling. He was afraid she would get up and run away.

"I'm sorry," she mumbled and he could see her cheeks flaming. "I didn't mean to embarrass you. I'm sorry." She picked up her handbag and began to search for something.

Brad strove for self-control. He knew how much he'd just hurt her. How embarrassed she must feel. He wanted to get up and pull her in his arms and comfort her. Her full lower lip trembled, despite her efforts to grip it with her teeth. How could he be so cruel?

Suddenly Brad's stomach did a painful flip as the realization hit him. This was what he'd done to Ann. He'd invited her for dinner in order to tell her it was over between them and here he was, getting ready to do the same to Katharine.

Brad cursed himself. What kind of a low life form was he? It hadn't been his intention to repeat that horrible scene. Only this time the woman he intended to send packing was someone he didn't *want* to reject. He *wanted* to love her. And although there'd been nothing explicit between them—except for his bumbling words and actions—she had just tried to offer her love to him. How incredibly brave she was!

His fingers curled into a fist. Not only did he owe her an apology for misleading her, he also owed her an explanation why he couldn't receive her generous gift.

Katharine, like Ann, had probably been expecting something totally different from what he was planning to deliver. He was a specialist in leading women on, and then taking them out for dinner in order to show them the door. Ann had run out into traffic, but at least he was pretty sure Katharine wouldn't jump overboard.

He looked at her across the table, and was filled with such a deep love for her he wished he could just ignore his past. Ignore any promises he'd made. Ignore what had happened to Ann and the baby. But the past existed, and he had to deal with it.

Now.

"Katharine, there's something I need to tell you."

He reached for her hand again. From its tenseness he could tell how reluctant she was to allow him to touch her.

"I'm listening." Her voice was aloof and as tense as her hand.

"Katharine, I owe you an explanation."

Just then the waiter came with their food and Katharine pulled her hand away.

They sat in silence. Brad found it hard to swallow more than a few bites, and he noted Katharine barely nibbled at her broiled trout.

After an interminable half-hour, Brad signaled for the waiter to come and clear away the food.

"The meal was not satisfactory?" the poor man enquired, looking at the almost untouched plates.

"The food was fine," Brad assured him. "I think we both kind of over-did it at lunch. Could you please just bring us coffee?"

With the coffee growing cold in front of them, finally Brad spoke. He hoped he could keep his voice steady, because this would be the most difficult thing he'd ever said in his life. Then, before he lost his courage, he plunged in. "I once hurt a woman very much. I was a cruel monster, and the results of my actions were tragic."

Katharine looked at him, her forehead wrinkled in confusion. "I don't understand."

He had to make a clean breast of it, even if it meant she would never speak to him again. Even if in her eyes he would forever be a child-murderer. He deserved that. Because he was.

His gut contorted with pain as he forced himself to look directly at her.

"Earlier in my life—I call it my pre-God life—I was callous and hard, with no regard for women's feelings. I never cared how deep their feelings were for me. My own were shallow, and physical love—sex—was all I ever wanted from them. I got plenty of that because..." He grimaced. "I guess I was considered good-looking by many women. Each time I moved on to a new lover, some women were angry or offended, but the ones who had confessed their love for me were deeply hurt. I knew that, but never felt sorry for them. 'Too bad, so sad,' I thought. I had warned them I wasn't into forever commitments, so they shouldn't have let themselves get too emotionally involved."

He paused, took a deep breath and went on.

"Ann was a beautiful, young woman and I knew she was very much in love with me. I didn't discourage it, even though I didn't return her feelings, because she was so good—"

He lowered his head. When he raised his eyes again, she was staring at him in horror. His voice turned rough as he forcefully ground out the words, "... in bed."

He heard her harsh intake of breath, but went on, flagellating himself mercilessly with the past. "She gave me the best sex I ever had and I didn't want to lose that, so I played along, pretending I loved her. But when she started to talk about marriage, I knew I had to put a halt to things. I didn't want to marry her. Why should I marry anyone? Life was great and there were plenty more women waiting to be added to my list."

He smiled mirthlessly. "Kind of like an old-fashioned gun-slinger. It's a wonder I didn't notch my bedpost. In fact, while I was playing Ann on the hook, I was quite heedlessly screwing other women on the side."

Brad looked directly at her, forcing her to listen to every cruel detail. He knew he was shocking her with his coarse language, but he wanted her to know the kind of man she was dealing with. "Sex was all I cared about," he said. "I was an unimaginably selfish brute."

Over the years he'd called himself every horrible name he could think of and "selfish brute" wasn't even close to being the worst.

He took a gulp of water to ease his parched throat and looked down at his hand gripping the stem of the water glass. His fingers were white.

"I took Ann to a fancy restaurant to break it to her gently." Brad laughed bitterly. "Gently? She thought I was going to propose. She'd got all dressed up nicely, and I could tell she'd even had her nails manicured, probably so her hand would look lovely when I slipped on the ring. I knew that. And instead I told her it was over between us."

That night was etched in his mind as clearly as the diamond he wished to God he'd offered to her.

"I'll spare you the horrific details, but suffice it to say her reaction was unexpected. To me anyway. Though if I'd had even a tiny bit of empathy, I would have expected it. She rushed out of the restaurant and ran out onto the street. She didn't watch where she was going and— she got hit by a car."

Here Brad's self-composure left him and his shoulders slumped. He pressed his thumbs into his eyes, but the tears forced their way out, wetting his palms. "The next day in the hospital I found out why she'd reacted the way she did. She'd been pregnant. And our baby—"

Brad got up and stumbled to the window and looked out into the black night. He couldn't say it. He'd never said those words out loud. Not to anyone.

Then he heard her quiet voice behind him. It surprised him there was no accusation in her words. "She lost the baby?"

"Yes." With one hand Brad wiped his eyes. When he'd collected himself, he returned to the table and collapsed into his chair.

Without a word, Katharine reached for his hand, and he clutched it like a drowning man.

Brad didn't remember when he'd felt this exhausted, but he couldn't stop. Not till it was all out. "I went to the hospital, but when she saw me at the door she began to scream. She didn't ever want to see me again and said she would never forgive me for causing the death of her baby—our baby. I'd never seen anyone in such a blind rage. It literally blew me out of the room."

He'd backed out into the hospital corridor and blindly stumbled down the hall and into the chapel, where Pastor Davey was working at his desk.

"I went into the chapel and blurted everything out to the pastor on duty. It was Pastor Davey."

Katharine's eyebrows shot up.

"Yeah, Sandy's father," Brad replied to her unspoken question. "That's how I met the family. Eventually I left my accounting job and went into theology. But in that chapel I made a promise to God I would never allow myself to love another woman until I had His forgiveness.

That way I could never hurt another woman like I hurt Ann. I know *she* can never forgive me—but—but neither can God." He choked out the last word. It filled him with inconsolable distress. "And because I can never have God's forgiveness, that's why I can never love you. I told Pastor Davey that will be my punishment for this heinous crime. Because of my callous behavior that caused the—the death of that baby, I don't deserve love. And I don't deserve God's forgiveness."

"What did Pastor Davey say to that?" Katharine asked. Her voice was gentle, and it seemed she was holding her breath.

"He told me everyone deserves to be loved," Brad replied. "But I know I'll never have Ann's forgiveness and don't deserve to be loved."

Katharine gripped his hand with both of hers. "Brad, maybe we can't always count on having human forgiveness, but I've listened to your sermons and it seems to me you've been saying God's forgiveness is always available to us, if we ask sincerely. Or have I misunderstood you?"

"That's what Pastor Davey said, too. He said God's infinite love is available for every sinner."

"And?"

Brad shook his head in dismay. "That's what makes me such a hypocrite. Sure, I've been preaching those words, but they don't apply to *me*." He pounded his chest with his fist. "My sins are too huge. I'm beyond God's forgiveness."

Katharine sat up straight. "Just listen to yourself, Brad," she said sternly. "You think you're so special that God has reserved some kind of a private hell just for you? You think you're not going to get the same treatment as all the other sinners on this earth? Boy, if that isn't hubris talking, Mister Too-Awful-to-be-Saved."

Brad raised his head while Katharine continued her berating. "If God forgives all sinners, then He'll also forgive you. You're just an ordinary sinner, you know, even if you *are* a man of cloth. In fact, I'll bet He's already forgiven you long ago. Probably since that day in the chapel, when you told Pastor Davey about your awful deeds, but you've just refused to believe that's possible and have been wearing a hair shirt to punish yourself. I imagine you've been sincerely praying for forgiveness a *few* times time over the years. No?"

She then went on more gently. "You just haven't believed that God's mercy and His love and His forgiveness applies to you, too. If we don't believe in that, what hope is there for any of us? But if you *do* believe that, then you can stop punishing yourself and live with a clean slate. And so, if you believe, then you're a free man. Free to love me. Your sins are null and void." She smiled at him.

Brad looked in wonder at this woman whose confident words fell on him like absolving rain.

"That's what Pastor Davey tried to tell me when we prayed together over the years before he died." He returned her smile. "Though he didn't use the expression 'null and void'. I just wasn't ready to believe it then. I guess I wanted to keep on punishing myself. The whole thing was too painful. It still is."

"Of course it is. I don't think that pain will ever totally go away," Katharine said, clutching the hand she was still holding. "It's something you have to tuck inside your heart in a special corner that's there just for the baby. Somewhere in the place where all the other regrets in your life are stored. But God has forgiven you because you have repented sincerely. That's what you've been telling others to believe. And I want you to believe it, too, Brad."

She took his face between her hands and said fiercely, "I love you, Brad, and I want you to feel completely free to love me back."

Suddenly a rush of joy replaced the pain and regret in him.

"Katharine," Brad's voice was ragged with emotion. She was so incredibly beautiful, so strong and loving. "Yes, I love you, my darling," he whispered passionately. "I can say it now. And it feels wonderful and right. I love you."

They sat quietly, gazing at each other. For the first time since the accident Brad was at peace with himself. The earth hadn't crumbled under his feet and a lightning bolt hadn't struck him down, even though he'd just told Katharine his horrible secret and had confessed his love for her. The past no longer had a grip on him. He was forgiven.

She took one of his hands in both of hers and kissed the palm. "Aren't you glad I'm such a good listener that I can throw your sermons right back at you?" she quipped.

He laughed, shaking his head. "You're incredible."

The lights reflecting from the water were making him dizzy, or was it the happy lights dancing in her eyes that affected him so? He desperately wanted to hold her. "I don't think we should be alone together again," he said.

"But—" Katharine stammered, frowning. "Why not?"

"Because I don't think I'm strong enough to resist you, now that I know you love me." He was teasing her and laughed at her puzzled expression.

"And?"

"I'm supposed to be engaged to Sandy, remember?"

The burst of Katharine's relieved laughter rang out in the night and mingled with a car horn from the street below. Even that sounded happy.

The waiter brought the bill. After Brad paid they rose without speaking and he led her outside to the deck where the lights from the dining room shone through the large picture windows. With his hand on the small of her back, he guided her toward the bow, away from the glare. There was no one else outside, and when they had reached a dim, secluded spot, they stopped. Wordlessly he pulled her against him and held her in a tight embrace.

"Katharine," he whispered and his famished lips came crushing down on hers. His need for her tore through him, and he relished the storm of feelings inside him. At last he was holding Katharine, the only woman he'd ever truly and deeply loved.

Brad gazed into her eyes and Katharine pulled his head down and kissed him so sweetly he almost melted. Then she smiled as she brushed the lock of hair off his forehead. He, in turn, released her auburn mass of curls and buried his hands in their scented richness.

"I love you, Katharine," he whispered and kissed her lightly. "I think I'm going to keep repeating those words all evening just to prove to myself that this is real. I love you, my darling, with all my heart." He kissed her again and again.

"I'm so completely happy," she sighed, resting her head on his shoulder. "I've looked for you all my life, and finally, *finally* I've arrived home."

"I've wanted to hold you in my arms ever since I first saw you," Brad murmured against her hair. For a long moment they stood in a close embrace, blended into a single figure in the dark.

On the lake a lone sailboat drifted toward the harbor.

"Brad," Katharine whispered. "There's a line in a song I never understood till now. 'This night will last forever.' This night is ours, forever. No one can take it away from us, no matter what happens."

"Yes, this night will always be ours, darling," he said, and for several moments he couldn't tear himself away from her aquamarine eyes. They were so full of love for him. Love he'd thought he would never have.

A discreet cough brought him down to reality. Some distance from them stood the waiter, inspecting his watch. Silently, he then withdrew back inside.

Katharine giggled softly. "Do you think maybe he was trying to tell us something?"

"I believe he was." With his arm still around her, they walked down the gangplank toward the parking lot where his car was waiting.

They got in but didn't drive off. Brad pulled Katharine close to him, not wanting to be separated from her by seat belts. He was surprised how his heart continued to glow with warmth. It was all so new and wonderful, loving this woman. After all those years of sexual philandering he finally was able to experience true happiness. The promise he'd made had always been like a life sentence he'd accepted as his deserved punishment, and he thought he'd never be free. But now he was.

"I don't believe I'll ever be unhappy again," Katharine murmured, snuggling against his shoulder. "Now that I have your love nothing can hurt me, ever."

Brad rubbed her hair with his cheek "I'll always treasure this night and the freedom it has brought me. Freedom to love you."

He kissed her then, hard and deep, and his lips slid down to the soft hollow of her neck. He wanted to continue down, down to where he could bury himself inside her.

"Katharine," he murmured brokenly. "You know I won't be content with just kissing you. I want you so much."

Katharine caressed his hair, his face, the nape of his neck. "I know. And I want you, too."

They sat, holding each other, until their emotions subsided.

"I have a confession to make," Brad said after a while. "I have been coming to the choir practices because I knew you were there."

"What? And I was in agony because last time you didn't even look at me," Katharine exclaimed.

"I didn't dare. I was afraid once I looked into your

eyes I wouldn't be able to look away, and then everyone would see how much I loved you. I *did* look at you
when you were concentrating on the music."

"I wasn't concentrating on the music. I was totally
lost and couldn't even find the right page."

Brad laughed. "That sounds familiar. I nearly lost it
the first Sunday you came to church. I guess you noticed."

Now it was her turn to laugh. "Noticed? I think it
was about as subtle as a sneeze. All that phony coughing while you were searching for your place."

"As bad as that?"

"Worse," Katharine assured him unkindly. "Everyone looked toward our pew to see who'd dazzled you
so."

Playfully Brad nudged her with his head. "They did
not."

It was amazing to him how things that had seemed
serious now were just amusing.

Finally, after many more kisses, and whispered
words of love, Brad started the car and drove up the
darkened streets.

"Please stop here," Katharine said when they neared
her building. "I want to make sure Maggie doesn't see
us. She'd be shocked and confused if she saw her
mother kissing Pastor Brad, after having witnessed
you and Sandy in an embrace."

Brad pulled over to the curb and switched off the
motor. He turned to Katharine and put his arm around
her shoulders. "I don't wish for Mrs. Davey to pass
away, but—" He sighed and shook his head. "I'm going
to find it very difficult to hide my love for you from
everyone."

"But what if Mrs. Davey expects you and Sandy to
get married before she dies?"

"There will definitely be *no* wedding. Except with
you. I'll think of some excuse if that should come up."
He gave her one more kiss before releasing her.

Katharine opened the door and slipped out. "Good night," she whispered.

With a final wave, he watched her hurry down the street.

Chapter Twelve

"Look, Mrs. Wilder, see what I brung you."

Katharine sat in a rocking chair while her pupils were cross-legged on the carpet before her, watching with intense excitement as she opened the packages that had mysteriously appeared on her desk. It was the last day of school and the children were jiggling with excitement. In a chorus they had insisted she open the gifts now, so they could see her reaction to each present. It amazed Katharine that no matter how small or large the gift, the children were always excited to see it appear from inside the wrappings. Hearing Katharine's thrilled comments made each giver squirm with happiness.

"I painted it myself, Mrs. Wilder," little Kevin said proudly as Katharine held up a small package wrapped in crumpled red tissue paper. Inside was a little green ceramic bear—minus one ear—painted with typical grade-one lack of accuracy.

"The ear kinda fell off when I smacked the bear against the table by assident, and Mommy was gonna glue it back on but I assidently dropped the ear on the floor an' my baby brodder got it an' then he wouldn't give it back. He screamed an' screamed so I let him keep it," Kevin explained.

"You're a very understanding big brother, Kevin."

"I think he ated it," Kevin added and Katharine tried not to laugh.

"Well, I think this bear has more character with only one ear. What should we call it?" Katharine held up the figurine and a chorus of suggestions filled the room.

"Green Bear!"

"Teddy one-ear!"

"One-ear Monster!"

"Yeah," Kevin decided. "One-ear Monster."

One-ear Monster was placed on the table beside the assortment of gifts.

"This is a beautiful bowl, Jillian," Katharine exclaimed, as she lifted a heavy crystal bowl from a box that had been professionally gift-wrapped. "See how it glitters in a rainbow of colors? I think I'll call it my Rainbow Bowl."

"That sounds nice, Mrs. Wilder," Emma said. "A Rainbow Bowl."

On the spot Katharine made up a chant and the children joined in, clapping the rhythm, while Jillian beamed with pleasure.

"Rainbow Bowl. Rainbow Bowl. I always wanted a Rainbow Bowl."

The final bell rang. As she said good-bye to her little charges at the door, Katharine marveled how most of them hadn't yet understood that they were going to be out of school for two whole months. Although Katharine had tried to make sure they knew grade one was now officially over, and she wouldn't be their teacher in the fall, this hadn't yet sunk in with everyone.

"See you next week, Mrs. Wilder!" Matthew called as he toddled past.

"Next *fall,* dear," Katharine called to the receding back. Oh, well, the next teacher could continue the battle.

She sighed. The empty classroom looked and felt

lonely. The floor was littered with the residue from the final desk cleanup. For a whole year she'd nurtured those little minds, and tried her best to instill in them the love of learning, and then suddenly—poof!—they were gone like so much dandelion fluff in the wind. Katharine wished them all a happy landing and began to collect her belongings.

Bonnie peeked into the classroom, arms laden with presents. "Coming to 'The Coffee Cup' after you get yourself organized?" she asked.

"Sure."

"Isn't it great to be loved?" With her chin, Bonnie indicated the many gifts she was holding in her arms.

"Yes, sure is." A flush spread on her face as Katharine thought back to Captain Mel's.

Bonnie raised a quizzical eyebrow. "Hey, I was referring to the little kiddies, not some hot Romeo!" she cried. "What's going on here?"

"Nothing's going on here," Katharine scoffed, turning her back on Bonnie's prying eyes. "I think you've been watching too many romantic movies. I'll see you in a bit."

She would have loved to be able to tell Bonnie about Brad, but she was bound by the Mrs. Davey debacle. When it was all over, she would happily let Bonnie in on everything. It was getting more and more difficult to keep her giddy happiness a secret from her perceptive friend.

She thought about Brad every day, and at night her lips throbbed with the heat of their passionate kisses. She desperately missed his strong arms around her, caressing her, and could hardly wait for the day when they no longer had to hide their love from the world.

She left the school, drove the few blocks to the small strip mall, and parked her car. As she headed toward "The Coffee Cup", she was so absorbed in her daydreaming she almost walked past the restaurant. It was only Bonnie's wild waving at the window that woke her up just as she was about to pass by.

The proprietor of the small, cozy café was popular with the staff of the nearby elementary school, and knew the teachers personally.

"Hello, Mrs. Wilder," he called as soon as Katharine walked in. "The usual for you?"

"Yes, Frank," Katharine replied as she sidled in beside Bonnie at the crowded table. "Though I really should order something different today to celebrate."

"You celebrating something special?" Frank asked.

Something special? Yes, indeed she was.

"The start of the holidays, of course," Katharine replied.

The teachers, all talking at once, were sharing their summer plans and telling funny anecdotes about what their students had done recently. The noise was over the top. Katharine sipped her coffee and nibbled on a piece of cheese from the platter Frank had brought for them as a farewell treat.

"What about you, Katharine?" one of the teachers asked. "What great plans do you have for the next couple of months?"

"She's going to be helping out at a kids' summer camp, would you believe it?" Bonnie piped up. "After working with kids all winter, she wants more of the same."

"Just for two weeks in August," Katharine amended. "In July Maggie's going to her father's for three weeks, and I plan to just relax."

And to love Brad.

Early on the morning of the bake sale, there was a flurry of activity downstairs in the assembly hall and adjoining kitchen. The previous evening some of the women had been at the church, baking cookies and frosting cakes and the delicious aromas still lingered. Katharine had made four apple pies at home the night before and they were now sitting on one of the long tables that had been set up.

When the doors opened at ten, Katherine was amazed to see so many eager customers surge in, each wanting to be the first to pick the best of the best. A white apron tied around her waist, she was kept busy boxing cookies, cinnamon buns, and pies. When she finally had a moment to look up, she noted her table was almost empty.

Maggie came up with a white cardboard box containing tarts and cookies, and placed it on the table in front of Katharine.

"Mom, could I have money to pay for these?"

"Of course, sweetie," Katharine said. "I have to get my purse from the locker room at the back. Could you just watch my table for me and help anyone who still wants to buy something?"

"There's nothing much left to buy," Maggie observed, coming around to station herself behind the table. "Just those rice crispy squares and a few oatmeal cookies."

"Yes, things have sold really well."

"Your pies sure went fast, Mom," Maggie announced proudly. "I was keeping an eye on them."

Katharine smiled. "Well, that's good. And I bet you can point out to me exactly who bought each one."

"Yup. Mrs. Hubble got two, and guess who bought the other two?"

"I couldn't begin to guess. There were hundreds of people here in the last hour," Katharine said over her shoulder.

"Pastor Brad got one and Sandy got the other," Maggie called out, triumphantly. "He said they looked just scrumptious."

Katharine stopped short and turned around. "Funny, I didn't even see them. I guess I was just too busy."

Brad hadn't come over to say hello to her. Katharine

hadn't seen him since the night in the restaurant and with no word from him, the longing to see him had grown more and more acute as the days had passed. Of course they had to keep their love under wraps, but still, he could at least have dropped by her table.

He also hadn't come to the choir practice on Thursday because there were only so many excuses he could use for stopping by. And he hadn't called her, for fear of Maggie answering. It would have required some creative lying to explain why he needed to speak to Katharine, but surely his need to hear her voice was as great as hers. It *had to* be! He had to be spending his waking hours thinking about her, and his nights yearning for her.

"He may have already left, Mom," Maggie said. "I saw him a while ago with Sandy. They were both carrying boxes."

Dispirited, Katharine walked toward the locker room where their coats and other personal belongings were stored. So Brad had been here and hadn't come to say hello. Of course they'd agreed to avoid each other, because after their ardent love-confessions it would be difficult to prevent their eyes from giving them away whenever they looked at each other. Yet even a quick greeting would have been better than nothing.

Once inside the locker room she closed the door behind her and leaned her head against the wall. She knew she was being silly, but couldn't keep her eyes from filling up. Having to keep their love a secret was so unfair. She pulled a tissue out of her pocket and dabbed her eyes. She'd found the man of her dreams, they were in love, but they were kept apart by some ridiculous excuse of him being engaged to Sandy. She stopped trying to keep back her tears and let them flow freely. No one was around to see her brief moment of self-pity.

The door opened, and quickly she straightened up

and composed herself. With the tissue she'd been clutching she blew her nose and wiped her eyes. Then, pasting on a cheerful smile, she turned to face the intruder.

It was Brad. He closed the door behind him and, with a strangled cry, Katharine flew into his arms. Her lips sought his, and she found them as urgent for hers as she could ever hope.

"Darling, darling—" he whispered, clasping her so tightly she could feel the wild beating of his heart against hers. As the murmur of his endearments mingled with hers, the ache and longing inside her dissolved, washed away by simply being in his arms.

Too soon he released her.

"I have to go," he said and began to search for something on the coat racks. He removed a beige cable-knit sweater from a hanger. "Sandy asked me to get it for her," he said. He gave Katharine one more quick kiss, and then he was gone.

Katharine stood, staring at the closed door, her heart singing with happiness. But before she could clear her deliriously joyous head, Sandy walked in. Katharine bent to inspect her locker key with great intensity to hide her flushed face.

"Hi," Sandy said brightly. "Would you believe I asked Brad to fetch my coat and he brought me this sweater?" Shaking her head, she walked over to the coat rack and picked out a short beige jacket. "Here it is. A jacket, not a sweater."

"He seemed quite confident the sweater was yours," Katharine said, hoping her voice was under control. "Would you believe, I put my purse in one of these lockers and now can't remember which one?" It was number twenty-six.

"Oh, the number's somewhere on the key," Sandy informed her. "Here, let's see." She took the key Katharine handed to her. "Right here. Number twenty-six." Helpfully she even opened the locker.

"Boy, am I stupid, or what," Katharine lamented. "Common sense should have told me that."

She emerged from the locker room, happily clutching her purse and walked back to Maggie.

"I was beginning to wonder what happened to you, Mom," the girl said. "I thought you got lost."

Katharine laughed. "I'm not that old yet. I just ran into someone."

"Mrs. Ericson?" Maggie asked, giggling.

"No, not Mrs. Ericson. Don't be unkind, Maggie."

"I saw Pastor Brad," Maggie then announced. "He just left with Sandy and your pies."

"Oh, that's nice," Katharine said. Her heart was still singing.

"What's troubling you, Brad?" Sandy asked.

Brad gave the kitchen counter a final wipe and hung up the dishrag on a cupboard doorknob. The Youth Group had just ended and they were almost done tidying up. "What do you mean?" he asked.

"You haven't been yourself," Sandy said. "You've been moping around and looking downright depressed. You lack sparkle. Tonight I think I could best describe you as a blob."

Brad laughed. "Gee, thanks. I couldn't have said it better myself."

"No, seriously, Brad. You've no wife to look after you, so I'm taking the liberty of pointing out to you that I think you're not well."

Brad shrugged. "I'm okay." He leaned his elbows on the center island, but turned his head so Sandy couldn't see his eyes. He knew she was the best eye-reader in town. Woman's intuition, plus, plus.

"No, you're not okay." Sandy leaned the broom she'd been using against the wall and came to stand on the other side of the island facing him. "Brad, excuse me for poking my nose into your affairs, but I believe you're in love."

Brad's breath snagged in his throat. How could she tell?

"See? I hit a nerve," Sandy said. She was too nice to gloat. "And I know who it is."

"You do?"

"Yes. And I don't understand what your problem is, my friend. Katharine is a wonderful woman and you could do much worse than marry her."

Brad felt a flush climb up from his neck to his face. He couldn't very well confess he was hoping Sandy's mother would die quickly so he wouldn't have to hide his love for Katharine.

Sandy remained silent, waiting. Brad didn't want to look at her, in case his eyes would give him away.

"You're right. I do love her," he muttered. "But—" He hesitated.

"But what, Brad? What's the problem?" Her voice was encouraging, and he couldn't avoid talking about it any longer. He knew she wouldn't let up till she knew.

"We have to keep our love under wraps, because—"

Horrified, Sandy struck her forehead. "Because of what I told my mother! Oh, Brad, I'm so awfully sorry I messed things up for you. No wonder you're looking so despondent."

"I miss Katharine," he muttered. "So much."

He knew he couldn't go on like this much longer. Having Katharine close enough to touch, but always out of reach, like the apple of Paradise. He wanted to announce their love to the world, but couldn't. He couldn't even snatch a few stolen moments with her because at home there was Maggie, and in the church there was the whole congregation. How long would this go on?

"How can I ever make this up to you, Brad?" Sandy asked, despair in her voice. "I'm so terribly, terribly sorry."

"It's okay, Sandy," Brad said, "This will pass. And you know, though I might be moping around, I'm actually happier now than I've been for years. At last I'm free to love Katharine. As you may have suspected, all the time since you've known me, I've been carrying a terrible secret that has weighed heavily on me and prevented me from being happy."

Sandy put out her hand and gently touched Brad's arm. "Yes, I knew something wasn't right, but it wasn't my business to ask. I'm guessing you shared it with my father, and if you'd wanted me to know, you would have told me."

It was time to let Sandy in on his past. She deserved to know, after all these years of being a stalwart friend. Brad straightened up and looked at her. "You know your father helped me to get into the seminary, but you don't know why I wanted to go. Why I *had* to go."

"You don't have to —" Sandy began, but Brad raised his hand to silence her.

"Yes, I do. I want to tell you everything. You've been like a sister to me, and I feel you should know." Before he lost his nerve he proceeded to lay bare his whole terrible past. He leaned his palms on the counter, while Sandy stood on the other side, listening.

When he finished, Brad was surprised and gratified to see compassion, instead of horror, in her eyes. Just as with Katharine. He could never have believed people would be this understanding and forgiving.

"I kept punishing myself and for years I refused to accept God's forgiveness," he concluded. "That's over now, thanks to Katharine. She made me realize God's forgiveness was there for me, too. Can you believe that I didn't trust Him? Me, who preached about it almost every Sunday?"

"That's wonderful," Sandy said, clasping his hands in both of hers.

"Yes. Because of Katharine, the weight of my guilt is gone." He felt so much more relaxed now. Once

again he'd experienced the power of human understanding and compassion.

"There's only one other thing I could wish for," he
said. "But that's never going to happen." He straightened up and went to put the broom in the closet. He
closed the door and turned. "So now if you see me
being unhappy, like tonight, you'll understand it's because I miss Katharine."

Sandy shook her head. "Because of my stupidity."

Brad could see her eyes mist over and placed a comforting hand on her shoulder. "Not your stupidity. Because of your concern and love for your mother."

"Thank you for saying that, Brad." Sandy went to
shut off a few lights in the hall. When she returned,
she asked, "You said there was something else you
wished for. What else is bothering you?"

Brad gave the already clean counter a sweep with
his palm. "Well, I always felt if I could have Ann's forgiveness, I could begin to live again with a clean slate.
However, I can accept the reality that it's never going
to happen. Even if Ann never forgives me, I have God's
forgiveness and that trumps everything."

"Couldn't you try to speak to Ann?"

"For a couple of years I tried, but she wouldn't even
let me near her. And even if she were now willing to
see me, what could I say to her that could make a difference? That I'm really, truly sorry a little life was
snuffed out because of my callous behavior? I've already said that, and she wasn't exactly impressed, to
say the least."

"That was years ago," Sandy said. "Things may have
changed."

"Why would they?"

"People change. They learn to forgive."

Brad shook his head. "Ain't gonna happen." But
something in Sandy's voice made him feel hopeful.
Was it really possible something could have changed?
How he wished he could believe that because now, for

the first time in five long years he wanted to live with a clear conscience.

Sandy placed her hand on Brad's shoulder. "Brad, I'm happy you confided in me. And if I can help in any way, I'll do my best. I owe you that much for messing up your love life."

He smiled at her dejected face. "Thanks. But I'm willing to live with the fact that you can't have everything."

They both started to head for the coat racks, but Sandy stopped. "Listen, Brad, do you want me to go and see Ann? I could explain to her you're a changed man and deserve to have this wiped off your slate. Where does she live?"

At her words hope, like a ray of sunlight, burst in his heart, but Brad quickly trampled it down. After all the pain he'd caused Ann, why should he be rewarded with her forgiveness?

"She could have moved to Timbuktu, for all I know." He tried to extinguish the tiny flicker of hope that wouldn't die.

"Don't you even want to try?" Sandy gently admonished him.

"Well, I don't see what good it'll do." He knew he sounded peevish, but he didn't want to let hope take root, only to be ripped out by Ann's refusal.

"Everyone deserves happiness. Even the worst criminals. And you of all people should know that, *Pastor* Brad."

"Sure, rub it in. You and Katharine both." Brad couldn't prevent a smile from tugging at the corners of his mouth. "And your father said the same thing, too."

Sandy pulled on her jacket. "It's been a long day and I have to get to bed. Those parents at Children's Aid won't be happy if I'm staring at them with glazed eyes while they tell me their problems."

"Well, at least you weren't napping when I preached my sermons," Brad quipped and opened the door for her.

As he locked the church doors, he could hardly recognize the strange feeling inside him. Hope was trying to gain a foothold in his heart.

Chapter Thirteen

"Maggie, remember when I used to take you to that park on hot, humid days like this?"

Katharine stood by the window, looking down at the park across the street, where the water-play area was full of squealing children, splashing through every sort of whirligig that could spurt water at them.

Maggie came to stand beside her and leaned her chin on her mother's shoulder. "Yeah, but now I swim in the lake when I'm at Daddy's. That's fun, too."

"Fun, yes, but make sure you follow the water safety rules, my Munchkin!" Katharine couldn't help feeling insecure whenever Maggie was in the water without her. When Maggie had been a toddler, Katharine had taken her eyes off her for just a moment at a public park and Maggie had fallen off the dock. A nearby fisherman had picked Maggie out of the water, choking and sputtering. Since then she'd had a hard time trusting others to keep an eye on Maggie while the child was swimming.

Was Ted vigilant enough?

"Your father's good at keeping an eye on you, isn't he?"

Maggie laughed. "Of course he is. He won't ever let us swim all by ourselves."

"Yes, of course he is," Katharine repeated, mainly to

reassure herself. "But you be careful when you're in the lake. Promise?" She smoothed Maggie's long hair and kissed the top of her head.

Maggie sighed. "Mom, I wish you'd stop worrying."

"So do I. But promise me anyway."

Maggie rolled her eyes. "I promise."

Ted was due to pick Maggie up that afternoon, and Katharine knew that although at first she would relish the freedom of no responsibilities, before the three weeks were up she'd be missing her chatty Maggie.

With the choir on summer recess and no Maggie to take to church, Katharine really had no reason to attend. Except to see Brad from far away, which could be more painful than joyous. And Bonnie had asked her to come with her for a Sunday brunch, now that she was a "free woman".

So Katharine didn't go to Sunday service and denied herself the bittersweet joy of seeing Brad in the pulpit. She missed hearing his voice and feeling the touch of his hand at the door, even for a brief moment. They hadn't met since the bake sale and Katharine longed for his embrace with an aching yearning.

That Sunday evening Brad called.

"Hey, I didn't see you in church today." His voice reflected concern. "Is everything okay?"

"Hello, darling," Katharine said breathlessly. "I'm so glad you called. Yes, everything is fine." It was wonderful to have him there, though only connected to her by his voice.

"I missed you. Why didn't you come to church? I can't tell you how disappointed I was when I looked for you and you weren't there, in your usual place."

Katharine smiled. "I'm glad you missed me. But since Maggie's not here, I went for brunch with my friend, Bonnie."

"Okay. But—"

Katharine started. He didn't know! Of course he didn't. They'd never discussed her religious beliefs and he probably just assumed she was a believer.

She swallowed. "I don't normally go to church, you see," she tried to explain. "And Bonnie would think it's pretty odd if I went to church when Maggie's not here. She'd think I'd been born again—or something." She gave a hollow laugh that was supposed to add a touch of lightness to her confession. "I'm not *really* a church-goer, you see."

There was an ominous silence at the other end that made her realize how her words must have sounded to him. Her legs refused to support her and she slumped onto a nearby kitchen chair, holding her breath while waiting for his reaction.

What had she just said? Was it even true anymore? In her previous life she'd been an agnostic, but now, having gone to church regularly and hearing Brad's sermons, she was beginning to think about God in a more loving and trusting way. Sometimes she even prayed.

At last Brad spoke but his words came out in slow motion, making Katharine shiver. "You're saying you don't believe in God? And you only came to church because of Maggie?"

"Well, yes." Katharine's tried to gather up her courage. "I told you that when I enrolled Maggie in the Young People's," she said, trying to defend herself. "Remember?"

"But if you don't believe in God, then all that stuff you spouted to me about God's forgiveness—you didn't believe a word of it yourself? It was just one fabulous Oscar-winning performance. Is that it?"

He sounded so sharp. So cynical. Katharine's hand flew to her mouth. God, what had she done?

"Well, I remembered what you always preached," she tried to explain, but her voice came out small and thin. "I was quoting you."

"If religion means nothing to you," Brad went on, "why did you bother joining the church? Why did you bother coming to choir? Why didn't you just drop Maggie off at the Youth Group meetings?"

She didn't like the ominous sound of his voice and she shook her head in despair. Before she had time to reconsider, she blurted out the truth. "I know it sounds crazy, Brad, but I fell in love with you even before I met you. At least I was very attracted to you—I mean your picture. Then, when you took my hand the first time, it made me feel so—so comforted and secure. And after that I've been coming because I wanted to be near you. I wanted you for myself. I couldn't help it. I was in love with you."

In the long silence that followed Katharine prayed like never before. He *had* to understand. He had to! Please, God!

He didn't.

"I don't get it. You've been coming to church because...? Run that by me again." His voice sounded sarcastic.

"It's true. I was first attracted to your picture on the wall of the narthex. I *know* that sounds totally ridiculous, and then when I met you in person I began to fall in love with you. And I *had* to get you to notice me, so I figured if I joined the church, and I went to choir and all that, you might fall in love with me, too." Her voice grew fainter and fainter as she became aware of what she was saying. It had never sounded that calculating to her.

There was a long silence and then she heard his voice, harsh and incredulous. "So what you're saying is you've been using Maggie as a front to entice me," he said. "Nice piece of duplicity."

Katharine's tears began to flow. "No, it's not like that!" she cried. "I joined the church so Maggie would learn about good things." In a way, it was exactly as he put it, but hearing him say it made it sound so much worse.

Katharine pleaded for him to understand. "I didn't

think I was doing anything deceitful." She covered the phone to hide a sob. "I wanted Maggie to come to church, and learn to be good. And I came to church because—because I wanted you." Yes, she had planned and schemed to get him to notice her, but it hadn't felt as awful then as it now sounded.

"Katharine, I just don't know what to think any more. You never believed what you said to me about God's forgiveness." Brad sounded hurt.

That realization tore at her heart. "Brad, I loved you so much. I didn't know how —" This time she had no time to cover the sob. "I didn't know how to get you to love me."

"So you set yourself up as an attractive bait."

He was right, of course. That's exactly what she'd been doing, even buying new clothes to make herself look sexy, but she had to deny it, in order to defend herself. "No, Brad, it's nothing like that!" she cried.

But it was. There was no way she could redeem herself, and quickly she hung up before the deluge of tears overtook her.

Slowly Katharine rose from the chair and in despair she began to pace the floor. She'd lost him. Just when things were starting to work out for them. She swallowed. Or were they? Would things ever have worked out for them, since she wasn't a true believer? In her happy haze it had never occurred to her to even think what kind of pastor's wife she would have made. The fact that she loved him and he loved her didn't seem to carry so much weight right now. She simply wasn't the sort of woman a pastor would, or should, choose for a wife.

Katharine threw herself face down onto the couch and her sorrow flowed out in deep, mournful wails.

She didn't know how long she'd been lying there, when all at once she became aware of the sound of knocking at the door. At first she was going to ignore it, not being in any shape to see a visitor, but then her ears picked up an urgent, repeated call, "Katharine! Katharine, open up!"

With a cry, she jumped up off the couch and rushed to the door. She whimpered with impatience as she fumbled with the chain that refused to obey her trembling fingers. At last the door flew open and she fell into Brad's arms.

"Katharine, my own darling. I'm sorry. Please forgive me." His contrite words fell like manna on her ears. Sobs racked her body and for a while she was unable to say anything.

Brad closed the door behind him and held her against his chest. "Katharine, please stop crying. I'm sorry I made you cry. Please stop." His fingers burrowed deep into her hair as he clutched her head in his hands.

"I love you," was all Katharine managed to say. Her heart, which had been in shreds only a moment ago, now, pressed against his, was whole again.

"I don't care what brought you to church," Brad murmured against the hollow of her neck. "I'm just glad you came. I can't imagine my life, never having loved you, never having kissed you." His mouth found her parted lips and he groaned. With his arms tightly around her, she felt the strength of his body against her.

Her response was immediate. Her limbs melted with sweet urgency and her head swam in seductive waves of oblivion that erased any lingering sadness. She forgot the church, forgot Maggie, and was only conscious of the heat of his body and his mouth against hers.

Brad picked her up and she wrapped her arms around his neck. He carried her to the couch where only a moment ago she'd been weeping, and now was welcoming his passionate caresses. Blood surged through her veins as his kisses searched for more of her, becoming more demanding and impatient. She responded with low moans. Nothing existed in the world but the two of them. He groaned her name as his hands found more and more secret parts of her curvaceous body.

Outside the long-awaited rain had begun to fall. Large heavy drops rapped against the window, slowly at first, and then thrummed with increasing power.

Suddenly a clap of thunder rattled the windowpanes and Brad jolted back to reality. Breathing heavily, he reluctantly released himself from her embrace and shook his head to clear it. He rubbed the back of his neck, trying to regain his composure.

"I must go. I only came because I realized how I'd hurt you. I wasn't planning to make love to you."

"Why not?" Katharine's voice was dark and heavy, and Brad wanted desperately to resume where they'd left off.

"Because, darling, with you I want things to be different."

"Different?"

"I want to make love to you as my wife. There has been too much lascivious behavior in my past."

Katharine gave him a languid smile. "Are you asking me to marry you?"

Brad laughed. "I guess I am. Katharine, will you—"

"Yes, Brad, yes!"

"Marry me?"

Katharine's voice trembled. "I definitely will."

"Thank you." He was relieved beyond belief. This was something he'd never imagined would happen to him in this lifetime.

"Brad, I must confess I'm not as strong as you. I want to make love to you whether we're married or not." She rubbed her cheek against his chest. "However, I'll respect your feelings."

Brad gazed down at her flushed cheeks and her lush, disheveled hair. He wanted her so very much.

"Thanks," he said hoarsely. "I appreciate that, because I know I'm going to have a hard time dealing with this."

He sat down beside her, wanting to enjoy her nearness for just a moment longer. It would be incredibly wonderful to make love to this woman, but not yet. Not till she was his wife and God had blessed their union.

He put an arm around her and she curled up against his side. He wanted to hold her there forever.

"Brad," Katharine smiled up at him, "I really do like the Sunday services. Not *just* because I love to see you, but I like the sermons, too. I thought you'd want to know."

"Of course I want to know." He lowered his head and rewarded her with a kiss.

"And I do pray sometimes," she said shyly after she was able to speak again.

"I'm glad. That shows you're thinking about God, anyway, and are beginning to trust Him. Otherwise, why pray to Him?"

"Yes, I think so, too."

"So you'll be at church on Sunday?" Brad asked. "I have to be able to see you. It would be intolerable to go for two weeks without even seeing you."

"Maggie's not home, so you could come—" Katharine began but Brad firmly shook his head.

"Look what almost happened tonight. I'm only so strong where you're concerned, my beautiful love. I'll keep away from here, but if you come to church, we'll at least be able to hold hands."

Katharine pouted. "Yes, for a second or two."

"I'll try to hold yours a bit longer. Maybe if we chat about some church affairs, I can make it look like I've just forgotten to let go."

Katharine laughed. "Sounds like a plan. We'll talk about the summer camp for ten minutes."

Gently he removed his arm from around her and got up. "I have to go."

At the door he again crushed her in his arms and muttered, "We'll be at the Youth Camp soon. I want you to know I'll find it very difficult, having you near me every day and not be able to hold you."

"Do you want me to cancel?" Katharine asked. "Because if you think it's better I don't come, I'm sure I could make up some excuse."

His reply was sharp and immediate. "No! I don't want you to cancel. Even the torture of seeing you every day is still better than not seeing you at all."

"I'm glad. Because I don't want to cancel." Katharine lifted her face up for a final farewell kiss that left her eyes sparkling.

A moment later Brad pushed the elevator button and felt like a heel, wishing for Mrs. Davey's quick demise.

Although she relished her three weeks of freedom, Katharine joyfully welcomed Maggie home from Bracebridge. She'd missed her chatty daughter, but now, after Ted had dropped Maggie off, the girl compensated for every moment of silence Katharine had endured.

As she entered the apartment, Maggie sniffed the air. "Ahh! You've baked cookies, Mom!"

"Yes, I did," Katharine said. "Welcome home, sweetie."

Maggie bubbled with enthusiasm, bringing her mother up to date on every detail of her stay, and filling her in on all the funny antics of her two little sisters. Katharine tried to quell the twinge of jealousy that always came over her whenever Maggie talked about her siblings.

"Grace has a paper route, Mom," Maggie informed her. "And I helped her insert the advertisements and deliver the papers. She wanted to give me some of her money but she hardly earns anything, so of course I didn't take any. Besides, I was just doing it for fun." She looked at her mother for approval and received it.

"I'm glad you didn't take any of her meager earnings," Katharine said.

"So, when do you think we could move up there, so I can see them more often?" Maggie asked.

Katharine hoped that, being so busy chatting, Maggie wouldn't notice that her mother didn't reply. She could sense the growing insistence in the girl's perpetual question and she realized it was becoming more and more possible that, as she got older, Maggie might one day want to move in with her father.

Maggie stretched deliciously and reached for her duffel bag. "It sure is good to be home again."

At these words Katharine's heart gave a joyful leap. Maggie didn't *really* want to move up north after all. Katharine pulled Maggie's purple suitcase into the bedroom.

"I got an email from Sandy while I was at Dad's," Maggie announced as she dragged her duffel bag into her room. "There was also a couple of words from Pastor Scott in the same message." She proceeded to pull out one soiled piece of clothing after another.

"Oh?"

"Yeah, he was at Sandy's and saw my email. I guess he was there spending an evening with his ladylove," Maggie went on. "You know how love-birds are."

Yes, Katharine knew exactly how lovebirds were. Her body melted at the memory of his passionate kisses and her throat choked up with longing.

Maggie looked around her bedroom. "My room looks great," she cried. "Those carnations are beautiful. Thanks, Mom!"

"You're welcome," Katharine said. "I think your room looked a bit greater before all that dirty laundry ended up on the floor."

"In just over a week I'll be going to the camp. Then I'll have to pack again," Maggie mused and began to empty her suitcase. "I'm starting to feel like a jet setter. You know, I could just leave most of this stuff in the suitcase."

"Oh no, you couldn't!" Katharine held up a tee shirt and a pair of jeans. "These clothes smell like a barn. Let's get all these stinky clothes into the wash."

"I just wore them yesterday when I went riding with Daddy and Grace," Maggie informed her. "They're not dirty."

"Maybe not, but everything smells of horses. Those stable clothes have contaminated all the stuff around them, so I want you to sort them into whites and colors and start the washing machine, young lady."

Maggie sniffed her tee shirt. "It's a beautiful smell, isn't it, Mom?" She laughed at Katharine's wrinkled nose. "Honest, I love it! If we lived closer to Daddy, I could go riding more often."

"Throw them in the washer," Katharine stated and withdrew into the kitchen to make herself a cup of tea to help her calm down. Couldn't Maggie just stop with this moving closer to her daddy business?

When the first load was chugging in the washer, Maggie joined Katharine in the kitchen. She sat down at the table and reached for two of the crunchy chocolate chip cookies on the platter.

"I'm really looking forward to going to church this Sunday," Maggie said, her mouth full. "I've missed so much stuff. I'll see the girls and they'll fill me in on everything about the ongoing saga of Sandy and Pastor Brad."

"Yes, I'm sure they will," Katharine agreed with an inward smile.

Everything but the truth.

"Wow! Two whole weeks here! That's, like, fantastic!" Maggie tossed her backpack into the air and let it land on the soft grass with a thump. For days she'd been ready to jump out of her skin with excitement and had spoken of nothing but the Muskoka Retreat.

"If I'm not mistaken, your flashlight and camera are

in that backpack," Katharine reminded her. "So you better treat it with more care."

"Oopsie." Maggie picked up the backpack and, heaving it on her shoulder, began to wheel her purple suitcase toward the main lodge. Katharine followed with her own luggage.

She'd feared her presence might spoil Maggie's enjoyment of the experience, but it didn't seem to bother the girl at all.

"I hope you won't think I'm intruding on you by being there," Katharine had said to Maggie as they were packing the day before. "I know you like to feel independent and —"

"Oh, Mom," Maggie had interrupted. "It'll be no problem, because I *know* you won't be coming around to snoop on me. *Will you?*" The last words were said in jest, but Katharine knew they were a warning that for the next two weeks Maggie expected her to keep her motherly distance.

"Of course I'll keep out of your way. I'll be too busy in the kitchen to snoop around."

She would have to keep out of Brad's way, too, because if she didn't, they might inadvertently reveal everything they were trying so hard to conceal from the church gossipmongers. In good time everything would be revealed. After poor Mrs. Davey was gone.

At a very noisy meeting the cabins were assigned. Maggie was to stay in one of the cottages with three other girls and Katharine, because she was helping with the food preparations, had been given a room in the main lodge close to the kitchen. As a camp leader, Sandy slept close to the girls' cabins, while Brad kept an eye on the boys' quarters from his bunkie.

The first week went well and Katharine, along with the rest of the kitchen staff, was kept hopping, preparing meals and snacks for the hungry campers. Each day began with a swim, followed by breakfast. Then there was a mid-morning snack and lunch to prepare, which were mostly served outside, picnic style. When the lunch was cleared away, Katharine had some time to herself, until it was time to prepare the afternoon snack and start supper.

Whenever Maggie was in the water, Katharine tried to keep a surreptitious eye on her from the kitchen window. She knew Maggie was a good swimmer, and the water safety rules were strict, but still Katharine found it difficult to relinquish the responsibility for Maggie's safety to the camp counselors. However, for fear of being labeled overprotective, she kept her worries to herself.

During the days she had almost no chance to speak with Brad. Seeing him gave her the bittersweet pleasure of being close to him, but at the same time she was filled with an acute longing to be in his arms. Even the fleeting pleasure of a brief touch was impossible, except in passing, when she was lucky enough to be passing him his meal. Sometimes in the evening, after the boys were in bed, Brad joined the rest of the adults in the dining area, which served as the staff common room. They gathered there for conversation and other pastimes, and Katharine usually chose to work on a crossword puzzle or play Scrabble with one of the women. Trying to sit close to Brad proved to be very difficult, without looking like she was maneuvering to do so on purpose.

That was just as well, for the sparks flying between them would probably have lit the whole room.

She kept an eye on Brad and Sandy, the "engaged couple", who
  often played cards together, and she had to keep reminding herself the laughter and joking were just acting their part. Yet, she couldn't help feeling annoyed that Sandy was able to enjoy his company while she—who was in love with him and desperately missed him—had to keep her distance. Life wasn't fair.

For a few days Katharine was able to put up with

the situation, mainly because after cleaning up and having a quick swim, she usually flopped into bed, exhausted. But as the days passed, the need to be in Brad's arms became almost unbearable. And since she couldn't trust herself not to show her emotions, she did her best to avoid him, while hoping this didn't appear deliberate. As far as she could tell, no one was the wiser. She always greeted him cheerfully at breakfast, and even had the odd conversation with him about camp affairs in full view of everyone.

Sometimes in the evening Katharine went out for a solitary walk or a jog along the beach, and the fragrant summer nights brought her a small measure of comfort. It was useless to hope for a deliberate "accidental" meeting, for she and Brad could never risk someone seeing them together, even to have a simple conversation in the dark. There were just too many eyes that could see them and start the tongues wagging.

One clear, moonlit night, as Katharine was returning from a jog along the beach, she rounded the corner of one of the cabins and ran straight into Brad's arms. For a split second they stood, in full view of the lodge, locked in an embrace.

"Oops!" he cried and laughed for the benefit of any possible onlookers, but his hands holding her arms sent electric shocks through her, revealing to Katharine how much he'd missed her.

"Are you all right?" He continued to hold her, making it look as though the collision had been forceful enough to unbalance her.

"I—I'm okay." Katharine brought the back of her hand to her forehead in a gesture that was far from being a charade. Her heart hammered and her legs were so weak she was afraid of collapsing on the spot. The resolve to avoid him was draining out of her like air from a pricked beach ball, and she wanted desperately to reach up and bring her lips up to his.

Brad's eyes glistened with dangerous fires in the

moonlight. "Are you sure you're okay, Katharine? You look a bit —" he began but Katharine cut him short.

"I'm fine," she told him—and to anyone else who might be listening. "That was quite the collision, Pastor. We'll have to start sounding a horn when we come around corners."

With forced laughter he released her and she made her reluctant feet walk away from him.

But this collision gave her something sweet to think about as she lay in bed that night.

The very next day, however, Mrs. Harrison gave her an even more wonderful gift. The woman began to complain of chest pains soon after breakfast. It was quickly decided Sandy would stay and conduct the Bible lessons while Brad drove Mrs. Harrison to the hospital in Rocky Harbor.

"Please could you come along, Katharine?" Mrs. Harrison pleaded, her face twisted in pain. "I'd like a woman to be with me. Silly me, I'm so worried."

Katharine tried not to show her pleasure. "Of course I will," she said to Mrs. Harrison. Even a few moments with Brad was a precious opportunity she would never pass up.

Soon they were in Brad's car, racing toward the highway with Mrs. Harrison reclining on the back seat.

In the hospital Mrs. Harrison was whisked off to be examined and Brad sat with Katharine in the waiting room, staring at the talk show on the silent television screen.

He was dying to reach over to touch Katharine's hand. To be thrown together like this—with no chance to even touch her—was excruciatingly painful.

Enough of this. Brad got up and went to speak to the woman at the volunteer desk. "I'm Pastor Scott, waiting for Mrs. Harrison," he told her. "We'll be just outside, getting some fresh air in the park area for a few minutes. Please call me on my cell when we're needed."

He gave the woman his number and then he and Katharine went outside to sit on a nearby bench, hidden by a row of shrubbery from view of the hospital entrance. As soon as they were seated, Brad drew her close. He didn't ever want to let her go, and her face, glowing with happiness as she looked up at him, told him she felt the same. She raised her lips up to his and Brad kissed her tenderly, deeply.

Katharine rested her head on his shoulder and sighed with contentment. "I've waited forever for that."

"This week's been a torment for me, too," Brad said, "being so near to you, and not being able to take you in my arms. To kiss you."

It was a relief to be able to speak freely without a dozen pairs of ears ready to tune in to their every word.

"Sometimes I've found it difficult to concentrate on the Bible lessons with the kids," he went on. "Knowing you were just on the other side of the wall in the kitchen."

Katharine smiled. "You could have come in for a cookie or something so I could have handed it to you. That, at least, would have been something."

"A tease, that's all. I think it would've been almost better if you hadn't come, after all," he said.

Katharine's face fell, and seeing her expression Brad squeezed her close to him with a laugh. "I said *almost* better, but not quite, my love. I still think seeing you every day is worth the torture."

Talk wasn't necessary. She said more to him with her eyes than anyone could have in an hour of talking. Brad continued to hold her, simply enjoying her nearness, until all too soon his phone rang and they were summoned inside. At the entrance they met Mrs. Harrison who was smiling broadly.

"The doctor said it was just heartburn," she announced, obviously relieved. "I guess I have to keep away from those fresh cucumbers. I'm sorry to have put you through all this. Silly me."

"Not at all," Brad countered. "I'm just glad it wasn't anything serious. I'll call the lodge and tell them you're all right and then we'll drive back.

"And no more cucumbers for you, young lady."

Chapter Fourteen

"Mom, I know the Ten Commandments," Maggie proudly announced one evening, as she visited her mother's room after supper. "Test me."

"I'd have to have them in front of me to make sure you say them correctly," Katharine replied.

"Why? Don't you know them?"

"I used to know them quite well when I was attending confirmation classes but I'm afraid I've forgotten some of them," Katharine confessed.

"Well, I've got them right here." Maggie reached into her pocket for a thin little book. "We're going to have a competition tomorrow about the stuff we've been learning. There's gonna be two teams." She handed the book to Katharine. "And my team's gonna win."

Katharine smiled. It was so like Maggie to be fiercely competitive. "Okay, let's hear them."

Maggie started to intone in deep tones. "*I am the Lord your God. You shall have no other gods.* That's number one," she finished in her own voice.

"I remember that."

"*You shall not take the name of the Lord in vain.*" Maggie continued. "So how come we always say, 'Oh, for God's sake' when things don't go right?"

"It's just a bad habit," Katharine said with a twinge of guilt. "I think from now on we should say 'Oh, for

Pete's sake' or something like that."

"Yeah, let's do that." Maggie then went on and successfully rhymed off the rest.

"That's very good, sweetie," Katharine said. "You've learned a lot here at camp."

Maggie chewed her thumbnail thoughtfully. "But you know what's the coolest thing I've learned?"

"What's that, Munchkin?"

"Pastor Brad told us no matter how bad we've been, God will forgive us and love us. Isn't that neat? Makes me feel kinda good inside, you know?"

"That's wonderful, Maggie." Katharine caressed Maggie's cheek. "I hope you'll remember that for the rest of your life."

"Why wouldn't I remember?"

"People forget. Remember the Prodigal Son story?"

"Oh, yeah. That father was kinda like God, I guess, because he forgave his son and loved him even if he was bad. I think now I get it."

"That's good. Shows you're getting older and smarter." Katharine handed the book back to Maggie. "Hey, why don't you come with me for a quick swim before you have to go into your cabin? I feel so hot and sticky." She went to the closet for her bathing suit.

Maggie jumped up eagerly. "Great idea, Mom. I'll just get my stuff and meet you on the beach. But you know it'll be your fault if my team doesn't win tomorrow."

Maggie ran off, and Katharine changed into her bathing suit. She slung a towel over her shoulder and walked toward the beach, which was unusually deserted. The kids were obviously taking the contest more seriously than she would have imagined.

As Katharine stood outside waiting for Maggie, Mrs. Harrison appeared on the verandah and waved urgently.

"I'm sorry to bother you, Katharine," she called. "We're all out of eggs. I can't believe it, but when I went to the cooler, there weren't any. Silly me, I forgot to order them. We need them for tomorrow's breakfast, so do you think you could drive to town before the store closes at eight? I'm sure you can still make it."

Katharine glanced at her watch. It was close to seven-thirty and the drive to the nearest convenience store, on the outskirts of Rocky Harbor, took almost thirty minutes. She'd have to hurry. She ran into her room, slipped a loose shift over her bathing suit, grabbed her purse and car keys, and drove off.

As she raced to town it suddenly occurred to her she should have asked Mrs. Harrison to go and tell Maggie not to bother waiting an hour for her. Of course she hadn't grabbed her cell phone in her hurry to leave.

At the store Katharine picked up three-dozen eggs and then stood in line for an eternity. It seemed everyone in Rocky Harbor had last minute shopping to do that night. As she drove back, dark clouds were beginning to gather, and before she reached the lodge, a fierce zap of lightning tore open the skies. It was followed closely by a deafening clap of thunder. Rain began to pelt down, hitting the roof of the car like small hail.

Katharine held the cartons against her chest as she ran into the lodge. She deposited the eggs on the kitchen counter, the water from her hair and dress dripping onto the floor.

"You must have swum to the store instead of driving," Mrs. Harrison joked. "You're drenched."

"Speaking of swimming," Katharine said, "I better go and apologize to Maggie."

She ran across the yard to the cabin Maggie shared with the three other girls and knocked on the door. Without waiting for an answer she quickly slipped inside to get out of the rain. She shook her hair and created puddles on the floor.

"One way to wash your floor, girls," she said laughing.

"Could you please get a mop so I can wipe this off?"

Three girls, lying on their bunks, looked up from their books.

"Hi, Mrs. Wilder," they said in a chorus. One of them hopped down to get a mop.

It took Katharine a second or two to realize Maggie wasn't among them.

"Where's Maggie?" she asked.

The girls looked at her with blank expressions, and Katharine's stomach began to sink toward the wet floorboards.

"I thought Maggie went swimming with you. She said she was," Paula informed her.

"Oh, God!" Katharine's felt the color drain off her face. She grasped the doorframe for support as her rubbery legs almost gave out on her. For a split second her mind refused to accept what she'd just heard. Then the realization hit her with the force of a lightning bolt. Maggie had gone swimming by herself and she hadn't returned.

"Oh, God, no!" she gasped and dashed out of the cabin. She ran toward the beach. On the dock, she almost stumbled on Maggie's sodden towel that lay there in a heap. With a moan, she picked it up and clutched it against her breast. Maggie *couldn't* have gone swimming by herself. She wouldn't do stupid things like that. She knew the rules.

Maybe she was in one of the other cabins. In a frenzy, Katharine burst into the next cabin, scaring the girls. No Maggie. She sent the girls off to check every cabin, and before long everyone from the camp had joined in the search. No one had seen Maggie.

Katharine turned and ran back toward the beach. Her tears mingled with the whipping rain. The waves were crashing against the dock sending the rowboats rocking crazily.

"Maggie!" she shouted into the storm and waded into the water till she was up to her waist in the lashing surf. She tried to make her shouts rise above the howling wind, but it swept the words out of her mouth and threw them back against her face.

Katharine waded farther and farther. A squall caught the top of a wave and flung it sharply into her eyes. Sputtering, she wiped her face, and lost her footing on the slippery stones.

The angry waters buffeted her about, but then strong hands grasped her and pulled her toward the shore.

"No! No!" Katharine screamed, struggling and striking with her fists at her would-be rescuer. "I have to go and find Maggie! Oh, my baby! Maggie!"

The arms wouldn't release her. Through the howling wind she could hear Brad's voice from somewhere calling her name, telling her they would find Maggie. Then she was in his arms, sobbing, while he carried her to the shore.

Brad placed her on the dock, where she sat, hugging her knees, her body convulsed with shivers. Someone wrapped a towel around her and nearby she could hear voices making hurried plans.

"Little island first ... two boats ... flashlights ... life jackets —"

"I'm going, too!" Katharine was finally able to get her voice heard above the din and confusion, but no one paid attention to her.

"I'm going!" she screamed hysterically. "I'm *going*!"

Brad crouched beside her, his fingers gently wiping the streaming water off her face. She looked up at him. "I have to go," she pleaded. "Please, Brad."

"Of course you'll go, darling." Brad helped her put on a life jacket and led her toward the boats, supporting her when she stumbled on the ropes lying on the dock.

Behind them came Sandy and the camp counselors, carrying lifesaving equipment. Maggie's friends huddled on the shore, wide-eyed with fright, some holding onto each other for comfort.

Mrs. Harrison sat on an overturned canoe. "Oh, my dear God, this is all my fault," she moaned into her apron. "I shouldn't have forgotten to order the eggs. This is all my fault. Oh, dear Lord in heaven."

The motorboats were launched, three people in each. Brad steered one, with Katharine and Neil, one of the camp helpers, aboard. In the other, Sandy was at the helm, accompanied by two camp counselors. Katharine crouched in the bow, clutching a flashlight that failed to provide much visibility. The spray hitting her eyes made it even more difficult to see.

Raw anguish tore at her heart, numbing her to everything around her except the need to find Maggie.

"Please, God," she prayed into the storm. "Please, let Maggie be all right. Please, bring her back to me! Please, God. If you let her be safe, we'll move to live near Ted. I promise. I've been so selfish. I'm so sorry, Maggie! Oh, please, God, let her be alive!"

They tried to head for the little rocky island, but the lashing wind made their path anything but direct. On a calm day the trip would have taken no more than a couple of minutes, but now, buffeted about, and not sure where the low-lying rocks were situated, it was good ten minutes before Katharine spotted the outlines of the island. On the rock she saw—to her great joy and relief—a shadowy form jumping up and down, waving crazily.

"There she is!" Katharine screamed. She jumped up and almost upset the craft. "There's Maggie! There's Maggie! She's all right! Oh, God, thank you! Thank you, dear God!"

"Katharine, stay seated!" Brad shouted. He was having a difficult time keeping the boat from crashing against the rocks.

Katharine collapsed onto the seat, weak with relief. The tears that now streamed down her face were tears of joy.

Brad circled to the lee of the little island and was finally able to land.

Maggie scampered into the boat, looking like a wet, bedraggled kitten, and dove straight into her mother's arms. Neil jumped onto the shore to push the boat off, and leapt back in at the last moment. Cheers arose from the other boat, and then they disappeared into the storm, motoring back toward the shore, where the lights of the lodge shone like comforting beacons.

Katharine clutched Maggie to her breast and tried to wrap her life jacket and towel around them both. All the way to the shore she held the girl against her and only relinquished her at the dock when the well-wishers surrounded them, hailing Maggie like someone returning from the dead.

After the ordeal, the adults gathered in the lodge, sitting around the long dining table, drinking the hot tea prepared by remorseful Mrs. Harrison. No amount of talking by Brad could make the lady forgive herself, so he finally gave up and decided it would just take time for her to calm down.

As they sat quietly talking, he noticed that Katharine didn't say much and looked uneasy about something. Of course he expected her to still be shaken up, but she seemed to have something else on her mind.

"Brad, may I please see you in your office?" she finally asked, making no attempt to hide the request from the people around her. At this point, no one would think anything of it.

"Of course." Brad rose and led the way into the little office where they'd had their first encounter. This time he shut the door firmly behind them.

"What is it, darling?" he asked and came to stand behind her. Katharine turned toward him and nestled against his chest.

A rush of love for her filled him and once more he thanked God she'd come into his life.

At first she hesitated, but then began to speak quickly and firmly, looking determined to have her say. "Brad, it was my fault all this happened because I didn't tell Maggie to wait for me."

Brad interrupted. "Maybe, but it was also Maggie's fault for not following the camp rules, you know."

"Yes, but I promised God if He would give Maggie back to me I would move up north. I'm going to ask the school board for a transfer. And that's final. I don't want to talk about it and I don't want you to try to change my mind." She lowered her eyes. "I've been selfish, just thinking of my own wants instead of what Maggie wanted. She's been asking for a while now for us to move so she could be near her father, but I haven't wanted to go to the trouble of looking for a house, applying for a new job, and leaving my nice school and my friends. Totally selfish of me."

She looked up at him. "I have to move. I promised God I would, and if I don't keep my promise something may happen to Maggie." Despite the tears glistening in her eyes, her face reflected fierce stubbornness. "Even if it means I have to—to leave you."

With a sad wail she burst into tears and sank into the chair by the desk. She lowered her face into her arms and her shoulders shook with violent sobs.

A promise to God? For a moment Brad stood, stunned. That's what he'd done. He had wanted to punish himself for his actions, and he'd sacrificed his love life. He hadn't accepted God's forgiveness even though he knew, deep in his heart, that it was available to him. She, on the other hand, had bribed God in the midst of the storm, bargaining with Him—if you do this for me, I promise I'll sacrifice something dear to me in return. He had to convince Katharine that God wasn't into bargains, bribes, or deals. Nor into sacrifices, for that matter. His forgiveness and love were unconditional, just as she, herself, had told him.

Brad knew it would be difficult to reason with Katharine at this point and try to make her see what she was doing was unnecessary. He gently stroked her hair that was still damp from the rain. "My poor darling," he murmured. "You've been through a terrible ordeal tonight. Why don't we talk about this in the morning?"

Katharine raised her tear-stained face. "No!" she cried vehemently. "I want to talk about it *now*." She shook her head. "No, I don't. I don't want to talk about it *at all*. I've made my promise and I'm going to keep it." Again she lowered her head into her arms and muttered, "I just wanted to let you know."

Her muffled sobs almost broke his heart. "It sounds to me like you were trying to bribe God out there in the storm," Brad said quietly. "God doesn't take bribes, you know."

Katharine answered with a hiccup, but didn't raise her head.

"Sometimes, when we're going through some terrible ordeal, like you did tonight, we try to bargain with God. We bribe him into doing our bidding. And then, if everything works out the way we wanted, we think it's because we were powerful enough to convince God to accept our bribe. That's not the case. God has His own plans for us. Sometimes things work in our favor, sometimes not. And it's always *His* design that decides matters, not how we sweeten the pot when we try to bargain with Him."

Katharine looked up at him and her aquamarine eyes, brilliant with tears, almost drove him mad. He could easily see himself promising God anything not to ever lose her.

"Yes, but I *promised*," she said earnestly. "And that's different from bribing."

"Not really. When we promise to give up something, we're offering up a sacrifice," Brad said. "A sacrifice is basically just another way of trying to bribe Him. And, Katharine, God doesn't take bribes, nor does he want sacrifices. He just wants us to love Him."

If that didn't convince her, he didn't know what else to say to her.

It didn't work.

"After He's shown His mercy and saved Maggie, I can't just lightly break my promise," Katharine insisted. "He might not like that and then—what if something happens to Maggie?"

"His mercy doesn't *work* that way!" Frustrated, Brad raised his voice, but remembering the others in the next room, he lowered it again. "He doesn't hold our promises over our heads like some sword of Damocles when we make them in a moment of despair."

"But something terrible might happen to Maggie if I break my promise," Katharine insisted quietly, clutching her hands together in her lap.

"Nothing will happen, Katharine. It's going to be all right." He pulled her up and held her against his breast.

"Yes, but —"

Katharine's words were muffled as Brad kissed her tenderly.

"Now go and check on Maggie."

Brad stood by the window and watched as Katharine slowly walked toward the cabins.

He knew she was not convinced.

After raging all night, the thunderstorm spent itself by morning. The next day dawned bright and warm, albeit slightly damp, but the sun quickly dried up the beach and the sports field.

Later that evening, Brad sat in his office, trying to finish some paperwork. It was amazing how the campers had carried on with the day's activities, as though the storm and the near-tragedy had never happened. How quickly kids adjusted. In his own mind the storm was still raging as he thought of his talk with Katharine. What else could he say to convince her? He rested his head in his arms on the desk where just last night Katharine had laid her tear-stained face.

The campfire was long extinguished and the silence of night had replaced the boisterous songs, but Brad almost missed the soft knock on the office door.

"Come in," he said, but when no one entered for a while he thought he'd been hearing things.

Then the door opened slowly and Maggie peeked in. "Can I talk to you?" she asked softly, holding the door ajar so only her head showed between the door and the frame.

Brad rose to his feet, "Of course, Maggie, come in."

For a moment she hesitated, but then entered and stood in the small room like a fuzzy elf in her pink fleece robe and furry purple slippers. Somehow, although she was a tall girl, she now looked younger and smaller. Her hair was in one long braid for the night and she fidgeted with it, curling the end around her finger.

"How can I help?" Brad asked. He pulled up a stool and placed it by his desk, indicating she could sit on it. Then he moved his chair so they faced each other, and leaned one elbow on the desk, ready to listen.

With uncharacteristic shyness Maggie sat on the edge of the stool and heaved a huge sigh. She remained silent for a few moments, which made Brad want to smile. It was so unusual for her.

At last she blurted out, "I feel bad." Two big tears rolled down her cheeks.

"About the swim?" It wasn't difficult to guess where this was going.

"Yeah. About making my mom so scared." She looked up at Brad. "She was frantic. Almost crazy, I think."

"Yes, she was."

"And I could see everyone else was so upset and yelling, and I feel really bad 'cause I caused it all."

"I know you do, Maggie."

She looked at him earnestly. "I didn't mean to do that, you know."

"Of course you didn't."

"I didn't think I was being bad."

"I know. But I don't have to tell you this could easily have had a very tragic ending," Brad said gravely.

"Yeah. It wasn't smart going off on my own. But I didn't set out to be stupid or bad. It just kinda evolved, you know?" She chewed the end of her braid.

"Unfortunately that's how it is with many situations that end up turning bad. The person doesn't set out to be stupid or bad." Brad swallowed. He didn't want to go there. It was territory he'd been through himself. "Things just kind of evolve, as you said."

"I really *regret* this whole thing," Maggie cried. "I wish I hadn't done it."

Regret. Brad's own regrets lurched inside his heart. "You know, Maggie, the longer we live the more regrets we'll have about stupid things we do. I have a special place in my heart where I tuck away my regrets."

Maggie's cornflower eyes flew open with surprise. "You have regrets, too, Pastor Brad?"

"We all do. That's because we're human beings and we'll never be perfect."

"Gosh, you mean I'll do *other* dumb things I'll have to regret?"

"I'm afraid so. Although I think you're such a thoughtful and considerate girl you'll try not to do *too* many things that'll hurt others."

Maggie gave a sigh of relief. "I'll sure try not to."

"One thing is, I'm afraid those regrets will never go away, and we'll just have to learn to live with them. However, we don't have to let them rule our lives. And if we learn from the mistakes, then the regrets will lie there a bit quieter. And of course, if we ask for forgiveness, then that helps, too."

"I told Mom I'm sorry, and of course she said it's okay. I still feel *so* bad inside. I *wish* I hadn't done that to Mom."

"Have you asked God to forgive you? Remember what we talked about at the campfire about His infinite love? He forgives us no matter what we've done, as long as we believe in His love and forgiveness."

Believe. That's what *he'd* failed to do.

Maggie brightened. "Yeah, I remember. And I think that's the coolest thing." She sprang up from the stool and shuffled around the room in her big slippers. Her relief was almost palpable. "So even if some people do something *really* awful, like being a triple, quadruple puppy killer—"

Brad gulped as the knife slashed his chest, but guileless Maggie went on. "—or something like that, God will still forgive them if they ask sincerely and believe in His love. Right?"

Brad had to cough and swallow before he could force the word out. "Right." This child was hitting all the right buttons to make his insides squeeze into tight, bleeding coils.

"Tonight Mom reminded me about that Prodigal Son story. Remember when you told it in church? I didn't understand it then, because I didn't know about God's love. His *infinite* love. We learned about infinity in school, you know, so I know it's, like, totally endless. Can you imagine anyone loving like that? I can't. Except God, and maybe that Prodigal Son's dad. And I guess my mom, too."

His emotions were in a total upheaval, but Brad had to smile at Maggie's philosophy. "Yes, that's God's love, all right. And as long as you sincerely believe in that, it will always be there for you."

"I think I get it about believing," she mused. "Because when I was a kid I *sincerely* believed there was a Santa Claus. Then I found out it's a fairytale, so now

I don't believe in Santa." She grimaced. "Which is too bad, in a way. But God *isn't* a fairytale and I can sincerely always believe in Him and He'll always be there and love me. Even if I do bad things. Right?"

"Right, Maggie, He'll always love you."

Maggie yawned. "I feel better now," she said. "Thanks, Pastor Brad. I'm going to bed."

Brad came to the door with her, but before she slipped out, he reached over and gave her a hug. "Thank you, Maggie."

Maggie looked up at him, puzzled. "You're welcome?" She shuffled across the dining room to the outside door.

Brad looked out his window after her. Under the outdoor light he saw Maggie run across the yard toward the cabins with her open robe flying behind her like fuzzy pink wings. Like a little angel.

Then the little angel lost one of her furry slippers and stopped to retrieve it. Brad smiled as she hopped on one foot before she got the slipper back on and then continued her run.

He returned to his chair and sat down, his insides no longer bleeding. Now he understood what the words meant when he preached that people should have a child-like faith, because Maggie had just inadvertently given him a living example of this. It was even more clear to him now that all those years he'd never really had faith in God's infinite love. That night at Captain Mel's Katharine had mentioned hubris. She was right. He'd been proud, holding himself above other sinners and beyond God's love and forgiveness. Of course it was there for everyone! Now he knew what the missing ingredient in his life had been. Faith.

During the next few days everyone treated Katharine with kindness and consideration. She knew they assumed the scary incident was taking its toll on her emotions, but the reality was, she was in agony over her decision. It had been easy to be firm that night and defy Brad's entreaties, but now, as she faced the reality of life without him, she was growing more and more despondent. How would she ever survive?

As if to make up for the storm, the weather remained warm and sunny for the remainder of the week, giving the kids ample opportunity to enjoy the camp and all its facilities. They swam, canoed, water-skied and rafted to their hearts' content. Maggie, however, was far from satisfied.

"Mom, this is getting ridiculous," she complained one evening as they were on their way to the beach where the bonfire was being lit. "You're always hovering around me. You promised you wouldn't. Remember? When we first came here?"

"That was before you showed me what an unreliable child you are," Katharine said severely. Maggie had no right to complain, after giving her such a terrible scare.

"Aw, c'mon, Mom," Maggie whined. "I know I blew it, but don't you think I've learned my lesson? And by my bad example I've even shown the others not to ever pull a stupid stunt like that. So in a way I've given them a vicarious experience. A life lesson."

"Maybe," Katharine conceded. "But for you, that experience was anything but vicarious. It could easily have been your last experience."

But perhaps it was time to stop hovering, Katharine decided. She was too grateful Maggie was alive and well to remain firm with her. Besides, she was neglecting her work in the kitchen. It was time to hand the supervision duties back to the reliable camp counselors.

During the last couple of evenings the staff joined the kids around the bonfire. Katharine left after the singing, preferring to go to her room to read, or take a quiet walk, rather than stay for the noisy wiener roasts, and be obligated to eat another sticky s'more.

Although tonight was the last evening of camp, she again left the bonfire early and walked up to the lodge to make herself a cup of tea before retiring. The building was dark and empty, with just a small fluorescent light over the door giving off a faint glow. Katharine entered the silent kitchen, which had echoed with laughter and bustle the past two weeks. Not wanting to spoil the ambiance with a glaring ceiling light, she switched on the dim bulb above the stove and poured water into the electric kettle. She put a teabag into a small carafe and leaned her elbows on the counter to wait. Through the open window she could see the people on the beach and hear their laughter, but the darkness in her heart refused to let in even the smallest shaft of joy.

She was determined to leave Brad and move up north to live near Ted . She thought again of the evening at Captain Mel's, when she had told him they would always have that night. Yes, no one could take it away from her, but now the memory was all she would ever have.

The whistling kettle announced the water was boiling and as she turned away from the window to fill the carafe, she could hear the door of the lodge open as someone entered.

"It's just me in here. Katharine!" she called.

There was no reply, but the steps came toward the kitchen. Katharine finished pouring the tea water and then looked up to see who had come. The words of greeting died on her lips when she saw Brad leaning against the kitchen doorframe, looking at her intently. She continued her tea preparations with deliberate concentration.

"Katharine," he said. "I just got word that Mrs. Davey passed away last night."

"Oh, I'm so sorry," Katharine said. "Poor Sandy. So it was a good thing she decided to leave early to spend the last few days with her mother."

"Yes, it was." Brad walked over to the counter and

came around to where Katharine was standing, her tea preparations interrupted. "And also, I came to tell you I've received a letter."

He paused. Katharine could sense a tenseness in him, but his face looked far from troubled. In fact, he looked like he was trying to keep his excitement in check. He showed her an envelope addressed to him.

"What does it have to do with me?" Katharine asked, not taking the proffered letter.

Brad looked like a little boy, who had a happy secret he couldn't wait to share. "Read it," he said and she could hear the suppressed impatience in his voice.

She poured a cup of tea to steady herself and, lifting it to her lips, looked at him over the edge. "What does it have to do with me?" she repeated.

"Very much." He kept holding out the envelope.

Katharine's hand trembled as she put down her cup. She took the envelope, pulled out the letter, and unfolded it. The first thing she looked at was the signature at the bottom of the note. Ann. Holding her breath, she began to read.

Ann wrote that Sandy had been to see her and had explained how the accident had completely changed Brad's life. Then Ann confessed she hadn't played fair with him. When she'd suspected Brad was losing interest in her, she had deliberately got herself pregnant in order to keep him from leaving her. She apologized for her deceitful behavior and was truly sorry for her part in the terrible incident. At the end, she told Brad she forgave him for his part in the loss of their baby. It wasn't entirely his fault.

Silently Katharine folded the letter and slipped it back into the envelope. She handed it to Brad. "So now you have your desired human forgiveness, too. You're lucky to have a friend like Sandy go to bat for you."

"Yes I am. I never thought this would happen." He tucked the envelope in his back pocket and went on. "I also came to tell you I've decided to apply for a position in a little church in Victoria Harbor. I called them and they're very interested, so I'll send in my application as soon as we get back to Toronto."

Katharine didn't know what to say. Things were happening too quickly. She, also, would be sending a job application to the board of education, which included Victoria Harbor. It was a large school board that needed teachers, so she didn't expect to have a problem getting a position.

"I'm probably going to teach in Orillia," she said.

"So if we're both accepted and you move north with Maggie, I'll be right there in the neighboring town," Brad said.

He didn't have to spell out what this would mean for the two of them. Katharine wanted to throw her arms around his neck and rejoice with him. Instead she swallowed. "It doesn't seem right, somehow. My promise was supposed to keep us apart, and now —"

Brad raised her chin so she had to look up at him. "Katharine, it's all right. Your promise was you'd move up north, which is what Maggie wants. And you're doing that, aren't you?"

"Yes, but —" He was right, of course, but still she hesitated and shook her head. "Somehow it seems like things have worked out too easily. My promise to God seems almost trivial now."

"I know you made that promise in all sincerity, and it certainly wasn't trivial. But God has His own plans for you. It's not your promise that moves Him."

"Yes, but —" Katharine stared at her hands and said stubbornly, "What if I lose Maggie?"

"Katharine," Brad's voice reflected his growing despair. "Maybe you didn't believe in God before, but obviously, if this promise means so much to you, now you do. And so now you must also believe in His love and mercy." His voice was firm and full of conviction. "He *won't* let you lose Maggie."

Katharine looked up into his eyes. "How do you

know?" she asked quietly.

Brad reached for her hand and placed it over his heart. "Can you feel it? That's my heart beating with happiness, because God showed *me* His love and mercy. After all the horrible things I've done in my life, He still gave me you."

He took her in his arms and held her tightly. "I want to hold you till you believe everything will be all right. God is good, and He'll look after Maggie. He'll look after all of us."

At last Katharine raised her face up to look at him. "Yes," she whispered. "I believe you."

Brad covered her face with kisses.

But then she abruptly pushed herself away from him. "What about Maggie?" she cried. "We can't just get married and have her think we've been doing something behind Sandy's back. She'll find it very strange if her mother suddenly marries Pastor Brad, after she's believed all this time that you love Sandy."

Brad laughed. "When the whole story comes out, and Sandy leaves to be a missionary, Maggie will understand. And we can wait—though not too long, I hope—till she's accustomed to the idea of us loving each other. And then, my darling, we can be married."

The darkened kitchen hid their embrace and the noise from the campfire drowned out their passionate words of love.

About Karen Rossi

Karen Rossi (the pen name of Kaarina Brooks) has been a romantic since she was a child. She and her sister had their own "publishing company" and wrote about love-struck princes and princesses.

Today she writes grown-up romances where modern-day "princes and princesses" go through heart-wrenching relationship struggles before reaching their happily ever after.

She now also has a publishing company, Wisteria Publications. Besides romances, she also publishes kids' books and non-fiction works, such as a cook book.

She lives in Southern Ontario with her husband and kitty-cat, Lilly.

www.wisteriapublications.com
brooks.kaarina@gmail.com